a carol dickens christmas

a carol dickens christmas

a novel

thomas fox averill

*for the Russell / Freed
family, with the
celebration of friendship.*

UNIVERSITY OF NEW MEXICO PRESS • ALBUQUERQUE

Library of Congress Cataloging-in-Publication Data

Averill, Thomas Fox, 1949–
  A Carol Dickens Christmas : a novel / Thomas Fox Averill.
     pages cm
  ISBN 978-0-8263-5501-0 (pbk. : alk. paper) — ISBN 978-0-8263-5502-7
(electronic)
  1. Academic librarians—Fiction. 2. Christmas stories. I. Title.
  PS3551.V375C37 2014
  813'.54—dc23

                         2014001277

Cover photograph by Jupiterimages, courtesy of Getty Images
Cover and text designed and composed by Catherine Leonardo
Set in Bulmar MT Std 10.5/15
Display is Bulmar MT Std

For my mother,
Elizabeth Kathryn Walter "Tucker" Averill,
who, like Carol Dickens, sought refuge one dismal
childhood Christmas but gave her family holiday
after holiday of sumptuous food, thoughtful gifts,
and, the greatest of these, love.

acknowledgments

Thanks to early readers Marcia Cebulska, Harriet Lerner, Ladette Randolph, Ric Averill, Jeanne Averill, Tom Rosen, and Ellie Goudie-Averill, and to later readers Linda Brand and Alex Goudie-Averill. All of you helped me rethink, refine, and re-find my material.

Andrea Broomfield, of Johnson County Community College, was a comrade and advisor during my foray into Victorian/ Dickensian ingredients and recipes.

Washburn University, as always, has generously supported my writing these many years I've served as writer-in-residence. Research and travel grants through the office of the vice president of academic affairs and the International House helped me explore Dickens' London.

Closer to home, I had the privilege of visiting a rehearsal of Mariachi Estrella, and I owe a debt of gratitude for such a pleasurable experience to Teresa Cuevas. Beyond that, the Hispanic community in Topeka is a culturally thriving, artistic, and culinary delight that enriches my life. My colleague and friend

Miguel Gonzalez-Abellas has again helped me with my Spanish, though all errors are my own.

Thanks to editors Elise McHugh and W. Clark Whitehorn and all the rest of the University of New Mexico Press staff for support and hard work.

Most importantly, and as always, and in all ways, I thank my wife, Jeffrey Ann Goudie, for her excellence as a reader, editor, and partner.

stave one

saving the scraps

.

Scraps was dying. After Thanksgiving, Carol Dickens sorted through the trash to be sure her son, Finn Dickens-Dunmore, hadn't stolen bones for the dog. Finn was just six when they had made the trip to the pound. He'd found the most forlorn, big-pawed, chewed-ear, cross-eyed mutt to claim. "Maybe not all there, that one," said the director of the humane shelter. "But good-hearted. Not a whiner. Not a barker, either."

Though reluctant, for parents are always the true owners of the animal their child picks among those caged at the shelter, Carol and Caldwell nodded their approval. Because the dog looked so pieced together, a crazy quilt of a canine, they named him Scraps. Finn had always fed him scraps. Once, he stole a chicken leg from the table and disappeared to Scraps' pen. The bone lodged in Scraps' throat, and Caldwell carried him gasping to the car and drove to the animal clinic out on Highway 24, where Dr. Matt met them.

Matt Groner had simply reached deep into Scraps' throat and

pulled out the bone. His father lectured Finn until the boy cried, "I wish I didn't even have a dog!"

Now, twelve years later, Dr. Matt gave the dog regular injections. "For pain. We're not going to cure him," the vet said each time. They stopped saying *cancer*. Finn stopped feeling the protuberances on Scraps' belly. As the dog deteriorated, Finn gave Scraps his favorite foods—chicken, cheese, and tamales. Carol still worried about bones, not knowing that Finn sat in his room meticulously picking meat from bone by the dim light of his galaxy.

Finn's first stars were glow-in-the-dark, five-pointed monstrosities, stuck up in the shapes of the Big Dipper, the Little Dipper, Orion, and Pegasus. Back then, after lights out, his ceiling glowed. He lay in bed, peaceful with his crude creations, until he heard raised voices downstairs.

Caldwell left during the Thanksgiving of Finn's eleventh year. Finn ripped down the little-boy stars, painted his walls and ceiling black, and created a second universe. Whenever Carol objected, he stopped her with his incredible knowledge of the heavens. He was recreating the galaxy as it would have appeared from North America on the night of the crescent moon closest to the day of his own birth. He showed her an approximation he'd found in a book. He cut tiny points of stars and rounded planets from fluorescent tape and replaced his lightbulbs with black light. He painted his window shades black, creating an ever-present night.

"It's so dark," Carol complained.

"I have enough light to do everything," Finn said, and he had, for the past seven years.

Finn's loyalty to Scraps was both comfort and concern for Carol. His care showed him to be a kind and gentle young man. But when the dog died, how would Finn bear the grief? Would

Scraps die during the Christmas holiday? Before Finn finished the semester? He planned to graduate early from high school and leave for Minnesota, for Macalester College. He'd applied, been accepted, and even received a rare midyear scholarship from the music department, all without consulting his mother.

"Why the secrecy?" Carol asked. "Why rob me of a smooth transition, with graduation ceremonies, a leisurely summer at home?"

"I knew you'd act just like you're acting now," said Finn.

"I don't like secrets," Carol said.

"Even good ones?" asked Finn.

Carol had to admit that, unlike his father's secrets, Finn's were always pleasant surprises. Over Thanksgiving break he had cut his long, dark hair and overnight seemed to become the man he obviously wanted to be.

On the other hand, Caldwell's latest surprise had come in the mail just after Thanksgiving. Carol had ripped open the envelope to find another envelope, stamped, with Caldwell's address on it. The letter, in Caldwell's tiny scrawl, read:

Dear Carol:

As you know, I have always done my best to make improvements to this god-awful town. When the downtown center became my development priority, I believed in everything I was doing. Unfortunately, Topeka has too many citizens of small belief. In short, this city is never going to make the changes I envisioned, at least not in my lifetime. I am selling off my many properties—the rental houses, the downtown buildings, even the little piece of land off Auburn Road we bought together in hopes of building that little cabin, back when such things might have been possible for us.

I don't know your financial position, but I thought it might be courteous of me to offer you first grabs on the Auburn land and on my downtown building with the loft. The Auburn land will sell for over $2000 an acre, and I'd like to keep all 40 acres together, if possible. My guess is that you might not be in a position to acquire such a large parcel of undeveloped land.

But, as Finn will be leaving for college next month (and aren't you proud of his initiative?), I thought you might actually want to downsize a bit and leave your old Victorian for something smaller and more manageable. I can make you a very good offer on my loft. For old times' sake.

As for me, now that Finn is graduating and leaving town, I feel I can go, too. I've had an offer from some business associates in Tucson. Arizona is sympathetic to development. It's a place, my associates assure me, without the downtrodden mental attitude of so many Midwestern cities, where all excitement, even that of development, is suspect.

I am half-divested already and want to start the New Year in a new place with a new attitude. You know I'll help with Finn's move to college and all that entails. Please let me know in the enclosed envelope what your thoughts are about the loft and the land. I know this may be a difficult time for you— Thanksgiving and Christmas always have been—but I would appreciate your response before the New Year.

Sincerely,

Caldwell

Carol had put the letter and return envelope on the mantel, where she would have to raise herself on tiptoe to even see it. So many times she'd wished Caldwell would move away, but wasn't it just like him to complicate the holidays? He raised the questions she now struggled with: how long could she stay in her house, with its need for a new roof, with the carriage house nearly knocked over by cottonwood roots, with a lawn to mow in summer, leaves to rake in fall, a snow-crusted drive to shovel in winter? All without Finn. And the other big question: what would she do without Finn?

First, there was Christmas. Usually, on the second Friday in December, they would read a page or two of Dickens' *A Christmas Carol* over dinner. They would finish the book, with "God Bless Us, Every One," on Christmas Eve. They took their Christmas meals from Dickens, as well. They began with a dinner like the unredeemed Scrooge might eat, as though appetite were suspicious: a bit of beef, a blot of mustard, a crumb of cheese, a fragment of underdone potato. Then the Cratchit meal, when only appetite could compensate for thin resources: a small goose with sage and onion dressing, applesauce, and mashed potatoes, a pudding after, with a few chestnuts. They ate a Fezziwig meal, too, as though generosity could abound so simply in cold roast, cold boiled, mince pies, negus, and beer. Their Christmas Day feast followed the rich abundance of Christmas Future: turkey, sausages, oysters, a cornucopia of vegetables, cherry-cheeked apples, juicy oranges, luscious pears, and seething bowls of punch. Finally, on January sixth of the new year, the Twelfth Day of Christmas, Carol and Finn shared a bowl of Smoking Bishop and an immense twelfth-cake before they put Christmas away—the ornaments, lights, and cards, the candles, mistletoe, and wreaths. The tree would lean against the trash can, abandoned and forlorn.

Such had been their ritual for the past seven years; Carol was determined that she and Finn would keep Christmas just as well this year toward the end of the twentieth century.

stave two

christmases past and passed

friday, december 12

Carol put a rump roast in the slow cooker before she left for her job as a reference librarian at the university. On her way she stopped at the home of her former boss, Laurence Timmons, once so lively and quick, now wheelchair-bound after an accident that had severed both his legs at the knees. Carol quickly ran through her paces; a peck to Laurence's cheek, a load of laundry started, the trash to the alley, the dishes stacked in the sink. "Stay," he said.

"Too much to do," she said.

"For me, it's nothing much to do," he said.

"You could learn to do more for yourself," she reminded him.

"I'd miss you too much," he said.

Carol had told him that she would not keep helping him unless he did more to work toward independence, but she didn't want to tell him about Mrs. Cross. She'd contracted with the woman to look in on Laurence twice a day. It was to be a gift, to herself and to Laurence, for the holidays. Then Laurence could decide whether or not to keep the woman on. She started for the door.

"I miss you already," Laurence called after her. "We used to talk," he said as she turned the doorknob. "Now you're a ghost, you haunt me."

Carol turned before closing the door behind her. "We are all haunted by our pasts," she said and hurried away.

After the stop at Laurence's Carol was agitated. Fortunately, she had work. The university had awarded her a research grant; she had the luxury of her own study carrel—the quiet to read and write in preparation for a spring conference in London. Her large research topic was transition, particularly the slow, nearly indiscernible shift from the Victorian period to the Modern: she studied the turnings of taste, forms, and attitudes.

For the London conference her immediate subject was the semicolon. Its fading use—due to shorter sentences (and, she wondered, less complicated thinking and language?)—signaled a turning away from the Victorian splendor of Charles Dickens and other practitioners of the capacious novel. At the same time, she'd noticed, typefaces had become sleekly modern; all the arts followed suit, the most lamentable being architecture, which now seemed nothing but glass and concrete in square lines, height the only aspiration.

Carol enjoyed counting semicolons in spite of brow-raising colleagues, baffled administrators, and her puzzled son. Finn played trumpet, and Carol tried to explain her interest to him by using his musical vocabulary. Punctuation created rhythm. Like the rests in music, or the bars that separated one measure from another, commas, semicolons, and colons announced *how* to read. One early punctuation theorist suggested that readers pause one beat for a comma, two for a semicolon or colon, and three for a period, or end stop. "Punctuation conducts the music of language," Carol concluded.

"I've never been to a punctuation concert," he said.

"You've been to poetry readings. You can't detect punctuation when you hear a poem, but it's there."

She was certainly finding ample punctuation in the first chapters of four Charles Dickens novels—*Our Mutual Friend*, *Great Expectations*, *Oliver Twist*, and *Bleak House*. She wasn't surprised to find more semicolons at the beginnings of chapters; Dickens, after all, would be writing exposition, description, the dense language that painted character and scene and thematic nuance. Of the ten semicolons in the first chapter of *Our Mutual Friend*, eight of them appeared in the first 750 words; similarly, in *Oliver Twist*, Carol counted fifteen right away, then only four more by the end of the chapter. *Bleak House*, such a giant of a book, did not surprise Carol with its twenty-three semicolons in chapter one; such a lot of work Dickens had to do to create *that* world. *Great Expectations* saw a more even distribution.

By midafternoon, eyes tired and with the evening's meal to attend to, Carol shut her book. Perhaps the next day she'd delve into something modern, maybe D. H. Lawrence's *Lady Chatterley's Lover*. No semicolons on the first page of that straightforward book.

Carol locked her carrel and left the university. She drove to the store for a chunk of cheese and potatoes. At home she moved the roast from the slow cooker to boiling water, peeled the potatoes, cut them into cubes, and marched to the attic. She hauled down the boxes of wreaths, of Scrooges, of carolers, of Santas and menorahs, stars and crèches. Finn was still at band practice, but when he arrived home—usually around six o'clock—he'd help her set everything out.

Finn wanted to check on Scraps. As usual, the minute he walked into the house his mother called his name. As if it would be anybody but him. He stretched his "What?" to show his irritation.

"Get in here, Grinch," Carol said. "You know what day it is."

Finn walked down the hall to the dining room where he knew Carol would be sitting before a table covered with boxes—the work, work, work of holidays. "I'm not doing Christmas this year," he said. He could just see the top of his mother's head. Her hair, he noticed for the first time, was beginning to gray.

Her face was still a young person's, though, as she rose to his challenge. "Bad Who," she scolded him. "We'll keep Christmas this year as we have every year."

"You keep it," he said. He perked his nose into the air. "Especially if it smells like this. What's for dinner?"

"The Scrooge meal," said Carol.

Finn screwed up his face. "I'll go out for Sonic."

"You've always *liked* our rituals," said Carol.

"*You've* always liked them. How's Scraps?"

"I gave him a couple of treats when I got home." Carol opened a dust-covered box and began to lift out the green and red, the white and gold, of Christmas. "Go to your dog. Then come help me." She held up their worn copy of *A Christmas Carol*. "Our reward," she said.

"Don't you ever get tired of the same old everything?"

"Like Christmas? Like being your mother?" She put Caldwell's letter to the side and set a marble crèche on the mantel over the dining room fireplace. "I *do* get tired of a backyard completely full of leaves," she said. "And of asking you to rake. But I accept that as a ritual. You should accept rituals, too."

"*A Christmas Carol* takes too long to read." Finn crossed his arms over his chest.

"It's short for a Dickens novel."

"We could do 'Twas the Night before Christmas' on the night before Christmas. Short and sweet." Finn uncrossed his arms. Scraps whined from the back pantry where he lay on his mat, surrounded by the gloom of dusk.

"We'll read *A Christmas Carol*," Carol said.

"Later," Finn said. "Way later."

"A little every night," said Carol. "It won't seem long that way. I know you don't have a lot of time, what with leaves and schoolwork and music concerts."

"They're really piling it on," admitted Finn.

"Like leaves?" asked Carol.

"I'll get to the leaves."

"And we'll get to the Dickens," promised Carol.

Carol checked on the rump of beef she'd transferred from the slow cooker to a large pot, where it would boil until it shredded when nudged with a fork. In the back of the refrigerator she found her English mustards—a Colman Original and one with horseradish made by Cottage Delight. She opened the jars for the coppery smell. Mustards never seemed to spoil. She found the French's American for Finn, in its fat yellow barrel, and put it on the table with the others. The potatoes were next, already peeled and cut into chunks, soaking in a bowl of water. Carol added them to the boiling beef, then rummaged in her bottom cabinets for the Dutch oven she used once a year to toast cheese. She poured in a quarter of an inch of Wychwood's Hobgoblin Traditional English Ale—Finn liked the name and Carol liked the taste—then finished the rest of the bottle. She rummaged in the meat drawer for the white cheddar she'd bought and discovered half of it already gone. In the pantry Finn muttered throaty endearments to Scraps, who had no doubt wolfed down the cheese. Let the dog be happy; the remaining chunk would be plenty. She took the crackers from their plastic bag. She'd made them the night before, as she liked cooking even the smallest necessities from scratch, at least at Christmastime. Finally, as the ale began to simmer, Carol sliced the cheese to cover the bottom and watched it melt. She portioned beef and potatoes and crackers onto small plates. When the cheese bubbled, she quickly spooned it onto the crackers and hurried to the table. She and Finn dotted the meager fare with mustard and ate. The meal was simple, but nothing about it was Scroogey, except Finn.

The unredeemed Scrooge meal, as though appetite were suspicious:

Menu

A Bit of Beef

INGREDIENTS
Rump roast, moderate size
Beef broth, 14-oz. can
Salt to taste
Pepper to taste

Put the rump roast, beef broth, salt, and pepper in a slow cooker, on highest setting, and leave for the day. When you return, transfer to large pot and add:

A Fragment of Underdone Potato

INGREDIENTS
Potatoes, 2 or 3 Russet, peeled

Peel potatoes and add to the large pot to which you've transferred the roast. Bring to a boil and let boil until meat shreds when poked with a fork and potatoes are done (or, if you're Scroogey, leave them slightly underdone). Serve with:

A Blot of Mustard

Colman's Mustard (Colman's has been producing in Norwich, England, since moving there in 1850 and is often considered to be "England's Mustard") or;

Dijon, though Scrooge hardly seems the type to want a French mustard, or;

French's, though Scrooge seems even less the type to want an American mustard.

A Crumb of Cheese

INGREDIENTS

White cheddar, one small block (Cheddar is the name of a place, early associated with the cheese and the "cheddaring" process), sliced
Hobgoblin Ale

In a skillet or Dutch oven, pour a quarter inch of ale (drink the rest with your dinner). Bring to simmer and add slices of cheese. Just as the cheese melts, use a spatula to transfer them onto:

Crackers

INGREDIENTS

Saltines, or any other dry, white cracker, or make your own:
Flour, 1 cup
Salt, slight amount
Butter, 1 tbsp.
Milk, ½ cup

Preheat oven to 300 degrees. Mix salt and flour, cut in butter until mealy, then add enough milk to make a smooth dough. Divide dough in two and roll out on a cutting board with a dusting of flour. When very thin, transfer to an ungreased baking sheet, cut into squares, prick with a fork, and bake for 15 to 20 minutes until crisp and just turning brown.

Over dinner, Carol chattered about food plans. *A Christmas Carol* lay at her elbow. Finn knew she wanted to read far enough to get to the mention of the meal they were eating, when a disbelieving Scrooge tells Marley's Ghost that he might be nothing more than "an undigested bit of beef, a blot of mustard, a crumb of cheese, a fragment of an underdone potato. There's more of gravy than of grave about you, whatever you are!"

Finn ate quickly and grabbed a toothpick from the little holder in the middle of the dining table. "You see this?" Finn asked.

"I do." Carol smiled.

"If I swallow it, I'll be persecuted by ghosts," threatened Finn.

"A 'legion of goblins,' of your own making," she corrected him. She picked up the book.

Before she could read, Finn picked up his plate. "Humbug, I tell you. Humbug!" he said.

"Grinch," Carol chastised him.

Just *let* her try to pull him into Christmas. Finn put his plate in the sink and took the stairs two at a time. In his room, he flopped on his bed. Above him was the Milky Way, so many stars compared to the one star of Christmas fame.

Carol sat at the table nibbling her food. If Finn didn't want to read *A Christmas Carol*, at least he knew it well. She supposed she'd become used to dinners alone, quiet evenings, stillness stretching through the house like a damp fog. In another month he'd be gone. She did not feel self-pitying, just challenged.

After the dishes, Carol sat down with a glass of sherry and D. H. Lawrence. Finn would stay in his bedroom; the abandoned Christmas boxes would sit on the dining table, waiting.

Maybe Finn was tired of *A Christmas Carol* because he had such a Scrooge in his own life—his father. God, if Dickens had written about Caldwell Dunmore. Carol's mood curdled. Dickens would have renamed him, of course, something like *Cadwood Doolittle.* Carol could imagine the prose: *He was a selfish man, a mean, tight-hearted, clutch-fisted man, thin as gruel, just short enough to worry about his size, just vain enough to trim his moustache to as thin a pencil as he was, just pompous enough to include a self-addressed, stamped envelope to force replies to his formal proposals: first of separation, then divorce, and now divestment.*

What had she seen in the man? His confidence had been mere bravado. His clear sense of the future had been for his future alone. What he called "my life plan" had never included Carol and Finn. His seeming good cheer, his social grace, his desire "to be seen," he said, "by the people who matter," had masked the fact that he had no idea what really mattered. His financial knowledge had gotten him the job as vice president for financial affairs at the university and also propelled him away from the university, into real estate and development, where he could work with "movers and shakers instead of hand-wringers and bottom-liners."

Caldwell had left "the dead end of the university" and "an unfulfilling marriage, the tomb of a quiet life in an old Victorian house in a shabby neighborhood." He'd moved into one of his properties, creating a loft above the downtown building he rented to a florist. Flowers in hand, he saw Carol only on special occasions: Finn's band concerts, birthdays, and holidays. For Caldwell, domestic life was a humbug compared to his properties, his developments, his notion of "growing" Topeka, Kansas.

Humbug! Dickens would never write about such a man. At least Scrooge could be set on the path to redemption. Caldwell

Dunmore, ex-husband, once fellow employee, owner of real estate all over town, was unredeemable. Carol had tried to make peace with her failed marriage. Why, she wondered, did the one left behind tend to worry most about the leaving?

Carol had been left before; she had her own Ghost of Christmas Past. When she was nine years old, the year after her mother's death, her father had promised her the Best Christmas Ever! He always trimmed the tree and arranged presents under it on Christmas Eve after she was asleep. She would awake to ribbons and bows above the windows, to sills and banisters festooned with greenery. A floor-to-ceiling tree twinkled with lights, sparkled with ornaments, cascaded with tinsel. Frank Sinatra or Bing Crosby crooned their white Christmases, their chestnuts on the open fire, their winter wonderlands.

But she had awakened to silence and tentatively ventured from her room. The living room was bare. Her small heart pounded in her chest. Her father's bedroom door was closed. She wanted to leave it that way, but she couldn't.

He lay on his bed, clothed, his head over the bedside, his necktie hanging like the clapper of a bell. But nothing sounded, not even his breath. She thought he was dead until a small gasp frightened her. She jumped back, and her foot kicked a bottle. "Gin," it said. She'd been a good girl, many times, and taken his bottles to the trash. She would do it again. Then she'd wake him up.

When she opened the pantry door, three pint bottles in the waste can matched the one in her hand. She didn't remember them from the day before. She threw the bottle at the others with enough force to break glass.

Carol made toast, slamming dishes on the counter. She clattered the milk bottle against the glass cup. She went to the stereo and switched the dial from phonograph to radio; she turned up the volume just in time for a shouting announcer to tell her it would not be a white Christmas. She could not eat her toast. She could not drink her milk.

She waited until midafternoon before shaking her father's body and calling for an ambulance. After the sirens Mrs. Moriarty from next door rushed over, all warmth and smells, and told the emergency people that Carol would be with her. Carol gave them the name of the closest relative she knew—a cousin of her dead mother who lived in the next town. "He'll be okay," one of the ambulance attendants said.

He was, though he nearly died of alcohol poisoning. Carol was not okay for a long time. She spent that Christmas trying hard to keep from spoiling the Moriartys' dinner. She stayed the night with them. Mrs. Moriarty's final bedtime words were, "Merry Christmas, hon. You'll get this all straightened out."

Straightened out meant going to live with another of her mother's cousins, two states away. She saw her father only on special occasions—her birthday for three years, two more Christmases, a Thanksgiving, and an Easter when he'd shown up to take her shopping for the "prettiest dress in town." Then he was dead. "Suicide," some whispered. "Drank himself into the grave," others muttered. "What's the difference?" asked Carol's guardian cousin. "He's dead and we must get on with our lives."

For years after Carol disliked Christmas. Now her rituals helped her through the season. And Finn was resisting. She wanted to call her best friend. Freda always knew how to cheer Carol. But Freda was on sabbatical in France, where it would be four o'clock in the morning. And Carol's long-distance bill had shocked her into reason the month before.

Carol put down her unread D. H. Lawrence, turned off the

lights, and climbed the stairs. She checked on Finn. In the glow of his intergalactic screen saver, his arms wrapped protectively around Scraps, he slept. The old dog moaned, and Finn shifted, holding Scraps closer to him. Carol tiptoed from the room.

Finn stared at the stars on his walls and ceiling. As on many nights, he waited for his mother to check on him and settle herself into sleep. He was patient, in part because he liked his room better than anywhere else in the house. They'd moved into the old Victorian when he was six years old. He'd been fascinated by fireplaces, and his mom and dad had given him the one upstairs room that had one. He'd never been allowed to light a fire, but he could feel the air currents lift, sigh, and blow when the wind shifted or the temperature changed. Finn's fireplace was a stethoscope to the outdoors.

One day, in the spring of his fifth-grade year, he heard a rustling above the damper, a scratching sound like his mom filing her nails. A week later, he awoke to tiny mewling noises. The squeals increased in volume over the next two weeks, and Finn still didn't tell his parents until, from the smell, he knew skunks were nesting in his fireplace. His mom and dad called a pest removal company, who recommended a chimney sweep known to solve problems with squirrels, pigeons, possums, and other intruders.

Mr. Marble was an unlikely savior. He sat on the porch swing, his legs not quite touching the porch floor, as Finn returned from school one day. "Skunks, is it?" asked the old man. He stuck out his hand. "Harry Marble," he said, "ready for action." Mr. Marble wore a dilapidated felt hat with a bright red feather springing from the band. His teeth were crooked when he smiled, and his wrinkled face was paradoxically smooth—worn and soft at the same time, like an old paving brick.

Finn sat next to him on the swing. "You going to kill them?" he asked.

"You want me to?" asked Mr. Marble.

"What did my parents say?" Finn asked.

"What do *you* say?" The old man folded his arms against his chest.

"They don't even smell that much," Finn said.

"But they make a lot of noise, am I right? And they're night creatures. So they're keeping you up past your bedtime. And the older they get, the worse it'll be, I can tell you that."

"So you're going to kill them?" asked Finn.

"Let's see," said Marble. "Up past bedtime. Noisy. Worse the older they get. A little smelly. Describes teenagers, too, doesn't it? But you can't kill teenagers, can you?" Mr. Marble stood up and went to the porch railing. He leaned over, and his head followed the chimney bricks up the side of the house. "This the one?" he asked.

Finn nodded.

"No cap on it. I saw that when I pulled up. But you can't cap it when something's living in there. Did you hear her lining her nest?"

"I heard some scratching," Finn said.

"Tell me all about it," said Mr. Marble. "Then we'll go up and take a look."

Finn told him the whole story, from the scratching to the mewling, from those faintly urgent sounds to the loud cries and disagreements. Finn told Mr. Marble he *liked* something living there, so close to him, like a part of the world coming close. Except the smell was pretty strong. Then Finn reached into his pocket for his house key and took Mr. Marble up to his room.

When the old man saw Finn's pointed stars, he named each

constellation pasted on the ceiling. "You put those up your-self?" asked Mr. Marble.

Finn nodded.

They moved Finn's bed away, and Mr. Marble waddled into the firebox. "Whew," he said. He put his hands up in the chimney. "They'll soon rust out the damper." He showed Finn his crusted hand.

Carol appeared in the doorway. Neither Finn nor Mr. Marble had heard her come in the house. The old man backed out of the firebox and raised himself up. "If you'll show me to a sink, I'll wipe off the hands, ma'am," he said.

Carol pointed Mr. Marble to the bathroom.

"You shouldn't have let him in," she said to Finn.

His mom always worried so much. "He didn't kill me or steal anything."

"Ms. Dickens, I do not come to steal, but to remove." Mr. Marble took a CD from the inside pocket of his jacket. "Here's what you need. When they're gone, call me and I'll cap your chimney. The damper may be ruined, but if you don't use this fireplace, you'll be fine." He handed the CD to Carol.

"What do I do with this?" she asked.

"You play it," said Mr. Marble, grinning. "All day, when they're trying to sleep. They won't last long." Then he was gone.

So Finn heard Metallica for the first time. *Kill 'Em All* played from the time Mr. Marble left until Finn went to bed. His mom shuddered at the sound, "Like so many nails on a chalkboard." Finn was determined to like the music. The next day, a Saturday, Finn kept the music playing: when "Metal Militia" was over, Finn started "Hit the Lights" all over again. By the end of the weekend, the skunks were gone.

"I'm almost out of here, myself," Carol told Mr. Marble when the old chimney sweep capped the chimney top with a little tin roof over strong mesh.

Mr. Marble asked Finn if he liked Metallica.

Finn grinned.

"Keep it," said Mr. Marble.

"No," said Carol.

Mr. Marble waved her away. "I'll get another. It's not part of the bill." He handed her a small sheet.

"No charge?" asked Carol.

"I couldn't help but see your old carriage house. Even took a peek inside." He held his hands to his eyes, as though peering into one of the dusty windows. "I was just kicked out of my storage. I had space downtown, but they're converting to lofts. Some kind of development, my new landlord told me. We'll see about that, in this town. But I need space, and in a hurry."

"Caldwell Dunmore?" asked Carol. She considered Mr. Marble's proposal. The carriage house went unused except for storage in its attic. Finn wanted to be able to see the old man again.

"I'll pay you, of course. Fifty dollars a month. I'm putting nothing dangerous in there. Just ladders and brushes, a little tar, cement. The tools of my trade have not changed all that much in the past century."

"Fine," said Carol.

"I'll be back tomorrow, if that's all right. I'll provide a new lock, and give you a key, of course."

The intrigue of locks, of bolts and secrets, appealed to Finn. He watched Mr. Marble drive away.

"You can keep the CD, but you don't have to listen to it all the time," said Carol.

"You could buy me some headphones," said Finn.

"No," said Carol.

"Or you could buy yourself some earplugs."

"I want to hear what you're listening to."

She meant she wanted to *control* what he listened to.

That week Mr. Marble moved his equipment into the carriage house. Carol let Finn play *Kill 'Em All* once a day. She pressured him to keep at his trumpet, even though he wanted to switch to drums.

Now, in his last semester of high school, seven years after Mr. Marble's visit, Finn still listened to Metallica, usually after he saw Mr. Marble, older and not as active, bring something into or away from the carriage house. Each time Finn heard the music, he could smell, just faintly, the deep scent of baby skunks.

When Finn was sure Carol was asleep, he slipped out of bed and dressed himself in black for his nightly walk. Finn was not bent on mischief. He was not a peeping Tom, though he knew the muted night-lights of all those people afraid of the dark. Finn walked not to see, but to think. He liked being a shadow, a ghost, someone not quite seen. He usually walked for an hour or so, in all weathers—from the heat of Kansas Augusts to the bitter cold of its Decembers. He liked cold best, his breath billowing, a tangible trace of his life in the world.

The night of December twelfth, Finn walked north over the Kansas Avenue Bridge above the moonlit stream of the Kansas River, then east, over the Sardou Bridge into Oakland. He liked the river bridges: avenues Topeka, Kansas, and Sardou, and the railroad bridge, all paths from Central Topeka into North Topeka, or from North Topeka into the Oakland neighborhood. Crossing a bridge, the river flowing below, himself so high, really getting somewhere, Finn left one riverbank behind to find himself on another. Each of these distinct areas of Topeka—Oakland with its Mexican American community, East Topeka with its majority of the city's black minority, North

Topeka with its flavor of the Ozarks, and the urban mix of Central Topeka—were like different cultures, and most of the kids he knew from school never ventured from one to the other. Just after eleven o'clock, walking briskly down Division Street, heading west, he looked for the steeple of Our Lady of Guadalupe Church. All around the church, in well-kept, one-story homes, lived much of Topeka's Mexican population. Some were new arrivals, but most were the descendants of Mexicans lured to the city in the early twentieth century by jobs on the Atchison, Topeka and Santa Fe Railroad. These people—many of them the grandparents and great-grandparents of his friends at school—strung the best Christmas lights in town. Roof lines, gutters, fences—even the borders of yards themselves—would be lit. Statues, life-sized crèches, plastic reindeer, and pink-faced Santas adorned sidewalks, driveways, carports. Lights spelled out "Merry Christmas," "*Feliz Navidad*," "*Paz*," "Christ the King." In Oakland colors were bright, varied, chaotic, almost ill-mannered. Christmas here seemed to be a party, a fiesta of faith. Finn loved the contrast to his gloomy Victorian house.

He walked down Lake Street toward Our Lady of Guadalupe. A man shouted from a rooftop. "On! *Ahora mismo.* Turn them on!"

Someone obeyed, and a rainbow of lights cascaded across the housetop. The short man with a paunch struggled down the short slope of his roof toward a ladder. He carried the staple gun he must have used to attach the lights. The man reached the ladder, then looked back at his work.

"Looks good, Papa," said a female voice.

"Hold the ladder, *puta*," said the man.

Finn watched from the shadow of a tree across the street. The young woman who had been called "whore" moved through the yard toward the ladder but stopped.

"Hold the ladder," the man repeated, louder this time.

"Get down by yourself."

"The ladder is steep, *hija*," the father said.

"And you are drunk," said the daughter.

The porch light snapped on, and an old woman in a shawl came outside. The daughter, her face now lit by the yellow porch bulb, was Gabriela, Finn's friend from the trumpet section in the Topeka High School band. Everyone said she hadn't come to school that year because she was pregnant. Finn had wondered about her. They'd once gone to a concert together, when they were freshmen. Now her belly was so swollen she couldn't button her coat except at the top.

The old woman went to the ladder. "*Está fría, la noche*," she said, looking up. "*Ven.*"

Gabriela climbed the porch stairs. She turned. She seemed to wave. Had she seen him? He ducked behind the tree. She went into the house. Her father clanked down the rungs of the aluminum ladder, held steady by the woman who must be Gabriela's grandmother. Still, the father missed the last rung and fell to the ground, cursing. The old woman walked into the house. The man picked himself up and stomped up the porch stairs. On the third stair, his foot crumbled through rotting wood. "*Mierda*," he said. He lifted his foot from the hole he'd made in the step. He ripped up the loose board and heaved it onto the roof before he stormed into the house.

Finn hurried away. Gabriela had been good on the trumpet. She'd started playing with the hope of joining her aunt's maria-chi band. But her father would hardly let her out of the house except for school functions or church. She'd joined the school band so she could go to football games and band trips, at least. The previous year she'd missed rehearsals in April and didn't show up for the year-end concert in May. When Finn called her, she told him she was telling her father she was going to band practices, but she was actually working to make money. "To be on my own someday," she whispered.

Once, when Finn went to the flower shop in the building where his father had his loft, Gabriela waited on him. She asked him who was so lucky to receive a rose. "My mom. It's her birthday." He'd hoped she didn't know his dad lived upstairs.

Finn walked past Our Lady of Guadalupe, past more houses with more lights. He turned west again, went up the Branner Street Bridge, known to many as the Fiesta Bridge, above the railroad tracks, then down Fourth Street, across the many sets of tracks, past the Santa Fe Depot, under the highway, through the edge of downtown, and back to his Central Topeka neighborhood. Gabriela had been so huge. She'd probably have her baby any day. Finn was fascinated by the image of her: unbuttoned coat, mussed-up hair, the little wave of her hand. The more he thought about her, the more he was certain she had seen him.

monday, december 15

Carol looked forlornly at Scraps, who peered forlornly back, his black nose runny, his brown eyes clouded and more cross-eyed than ever. She put two dog treats in the bowl on the floor of the pantry and left by the back door. She drove toward Laurence Timmons' house, determined to talk to him about the new help, her gift of Mrs. Cross. Carol's once-rich friend-ship with Laurence had become reduced to the thinness of pity. Years before, when Caldwell left her, Laurence had taken Carol's side, taken her on dates, almost taken her heart. Then, his terrible accident and his battle for life came first; then the adjustment to the wheelchair; then, as Laurence said, "The battle to *want* to live."

Others had helped; their circle of friends shared evenings of food, drink, lively conversation about books and films and university politics. But Laurence tired easily. As his energy diminished, friends found it as difficult to be with Laurence as he found it difficult to be with himself. Within six months, he was reduced to a few loyal friends. Most-loyal Carol Dickens stood by him as his house filled up with magazines, coffee cups, and cats. His isolation was exacerbated by his inability—Carol called it unwillingness—to venture past his door. Weekdays, Carol had helped Laurence with his daily needs—some things from upstairs, some things from the kitchen, some tissues and salve, food and water for the cats. He never asked much of her. He'd been a good boss and friend. How could she *not* feel sorry for him? But, duty and pity wearing thin, she had to quit her daily visits. Mrs. Cross, an older woman, a former nurse, a matter-of-fact but kind person, would start the next day.

Carol walked into a house filled with roses, an incredible array of red and pink and yellow and white, in vases, on the coffee table, the dining table, the bookshelves. Some, still swathed in green tissue, lay on the couch, the chairs, the floor. "Took me two florists," Laurence said. "The second one ran out of vases. All I could do to keep from telling them what I was up to."

"And what are you up to?" Carol began collecting the unvased flowers.

"You can't ask, you have to say," said Laurence.

"Can I at least put these in glasses for you?" Carol went to the kitchen. "And then you'll tell me what this is all about?" she called out.

"You might count them." Laurence wheeled through the dining room to watch her. He gave her his contradictory smile—his mouth drawn down by pain and persistence, his eyes clear blue and sparkling, forehead wrinkled with happiness. "They're for you," he said. "One for each day you've come over to help. I haven't thanked you enough."

"So you do it all at once?" Carol chided him.

Laurence held out his arms, and she came to him. As a short person, she hardly bent to give the seated man a quick hug.

"You were ready to break my heart," he said. "Mrs. Cross, indeed."

Carol raised her eyebrows.

"She called. 'For an inventory,' she said. Cleaning supplies, food. She drinks nothing but oolong tea."

Carol walked into the living room. The blinds were barely open. The room was sepia. A cat stretched.

"Why didn't you want to talk it out?" Laurence wheeled into the room. "Your needs and mine? My disability against your ability? Your disability against my ability? You think our relationship is one-sided."

Carol said nothing.

"The roses are us," Laurence said. "We, together. They're not about single days, they're about *accumulation*. I wanted you to see how affection has grown in my heart."

"While I've grown thorns in mine?" Carol asked. Wasn't that his implication? That she was ready to abandon him, to ignore their friendship, because she feared deepening their relationship?

Laurence wheeled to her. "You think I'm the thorn. The thorn in your side." He took her hand. "You're the petal of the rose, Carol."

Carol pulled away from him. "I need to concentrate," she said. "Finn will be gone. Soon. He's distant. I want to focus on him, give him something before he leaves next month."

"Why not give him some happiness?" asked Laurence. "Though I guess you'd have to start *being* happy first."

"Are *you* happy?" Carol asked him. She swept her arm across the room. Underneath the dozens and dozens of roses was the detritus of newspapers and magazines, the dust-covered books, the stained dining table. She knew the molds and messes of his kitchen, the bathroom stains, the peeling paint in the mud room, the cracks in the ceiling plaster, the random burned-out light-bulbs. The roses declared his feelings. The rest declared everything he'd let go.

"All this time, and you still can't imagine," he said.

"Imagine what?"

"This." He cupped the stumps of his legs with his hands. He laughed. "I can't stand it that I can't stand."

Carol shuddered each time she imagined the accident: Laurence walking between two parked cars, one of them suddenly hit from behind, pinching his legs just at the knees between two bumpers coincidentally the same height. She saw him crumpled, stuck, waiting for help.

"I can't stand. And you can't *under*stand," Laurence said.

"Which doctor said you might stand?" Carol asked him. "Which one wants you to go with prostheses?"

"He couldn't *promise* anything," Laurence reminded her.

Carol walked directly to his chair and this time kneeled in front of him. "Who can promise anything?" she said.

"You could," he said. "And perhaps I could make promises, too?" He reached out and touched her cheek, patted her salt-and-pepper hair, rested his hand on her thin shoulder.

Laurence had almost died from blood loss. His recovery had been tedious. Not only had he lost blood and strength, but by the time he started his rehabilitation, his weakened muscles cramped with pain. "Everything is so hard," he had often reminded her. He was a baby in his needs. "Toileting, bathing, feeding, dressing. I'm glad Maude and I had no children. Can you imagine a child taking care of a baby like me?"

Carol had mothered Laurence as best she could. "If you're a baby, give yourself a baby's timetable," she had suggested. "You're already talking, so you'll feed yourself, you'll even master toileting."

"But won't walk," he had reminded her.

Now Carol stood up with a welter of emotions. She had been helping him through a bad patch, just as he'd helped her through her divorce. She'd imagined loving him; she enjoyed his wit, his voracious appetite for books, his empathy. But love had been replaced by frustration: she was as sorry for his *disability* as she was angry that he didn't try for more *ability*—physical therapy, prostheses, a hand-operated car. She looked at the door.

Laurence followed her gaze and her thinking. "When I'm with you," he said, "I see roses, not thorns. I thank you for that."

Carol sighed. "I see everything. Including thorns *and* difficulties. I need to get to work."

"Still counting semicolons?"

"Don't you *dare* make fun of me," said Carol. She went for her purse.

"I'm just asking you to count roses, as well. Could be I'm on the verge of one of your transitions." He wheeled toward a vase. "I have a suggestion."

"You have a room full of suggestions."

"Study Gertrude Stein," said Laurence. "She wrote without punctuation. You'd have more time with what I hope will be the new me."

"Why would anyone give up punctuation?" Carol muttered. "I mean, if you didn't have to? Why decrease your range, your amplification, your connections, your subtlety? You'd cripple your abilities with the language."

"Almost as bad as having no legs?"

"You were in an accident," said Carol. "Gertrude Stein crippled herself through an act of will." She walked toward the door. "Does the new you plan to give up the wheelchair? Get off disability and go back to your job?"

"You could be director. You'd be good."

"I don't want your job. I want *you* back at your job." Carol looked past him one last time. "You don't have to live like this." She started out the door.

"I have promise," Laurence called after her. "I have promises. For you!"

Carol hurried into the chill of the day. She walked down the porch stairs rather than the ramp Laurence's handyman had built. She drove away without looking back. She did not want to see Laurence, who had no doubt wheeled his chair onto the porch to practice his phony Miss America wave, elbow raised, his entire arm rotating. In his lap, a single rose. Even though the day was bitter, her cheeks burned.

Finn left school after third period. He had two independent studies, for trumpet practice, and seniors had a lot of freedom, especially if they were good students and had fulfilled their graduation requirements, as Finn had. He walked in the cold, his sweatshirt hood tied tight, his hands in uncharacteristic gloves, heading for an early lunch at Rosaria's, where all of December they made tamales—pork, beef, chicken, and special dessert tamales with raisins and nuts. On the way, he passed Gabriela's house. No lamps shone in the windows. The holiday bulbs on the guttering and roof were not lit. In daylight the house showed its age and neglect: peeling paint, chewed window trimmings, the missing porch stair still on the crumbling roof. And one thing he hadn't noticed the Friday before: a for sale sign.

Gabriela appeared on the porch, looking happy to see him. "Did you know my father would be away today?" she asked Finn.

"Did you know I'd come by?" He came up her sidewalk.

"You were one of the okay boys," she said.

"I'm headed to Rosaria's," said Finn.

"She won't tell on me." Gabriela went inside for the long coat that buttoned only so far down, then hung like a cape. "Rosaria is my godmother," she said. "She says she's known me too long to turn her back on me like all the others."

Finn helped Gabriela hop the missing stair. "I didn't know for sure why you weren't in school," he said.

"You can see," she said.

"I saw the other night." He offered her his gloves and stuffed his hands in his pockets. They walked the four blocks to the restaurant without talking. Finn didn't want to pry. He didn't really know why he'd walked by. He sure didn't know she'd be waiting for him.

Rosaria greeted them warmly and started to seat them in a booth. Gabriela shook her head and pointed to her huge womb. "*Por cierto*," Rosaria said, smiling. "*¿Cómo estás, coneja?*"

"*Bien*," said Gabriela, "*y grande, y lista.*"

Before Rosaria could hand them menus, Finn said, "One each of the tamales, please."

"*Lo mismo*," said Gabriela. "*Y agua, por favor.*"

Rosaria hurried to the kitchen to shout their orders. Then she greeted customers. December was her busy month. Soon the restaurant would be full. Topekans loved her tamales. In the December cold nobody wanted to wait long in the lines that could snake down the sidewalk in front of her restaurant, so Rosaria bustled to be sure people were warmly seated, fed, satisfied, and then quickly helped out the door. Finn and Gabriela, shy with each other, sat and watched her. "I wish she was my mother," said Gabriela.

Their server came with water. Gabriela bit off the paper end of the straw wrapper and shot the rest of the tube at Finn. He put his hand to his face in mock horror. "Your father is selling our house," she said.

Finn took his hands from his eyes. "What?" He didn't know his father owned the property. "Why?"

"He's *your* father," said Gabriela. "You could ask him."

Their tamales arrived. Finn slowly pulled the corn husk from the masa. The steaming dough, warm, pungent, comforting, took his mind off his father. "My favorite tamale," he said of the chicken. He picked it up, wrapped it in a napkin, and put it in the pocket of his sweatshirt jacket.

"It's tamal," Gabriela said. "Tamales is plural, but tamal is singular. Unless you're totally gringo." She reached over the table and slapped his shoulder to show she was teasing. "But if it's your favorite," she asked, "why are you putting it in your pocket? You could get a doggie bag."

"It *is* for my dog," said Finn. "Scraps loves these more than anything in the world."

"We had a dog that liked tamales," said Gabriela.

"*Algodón*. Cotton," Finn remembered. "A little white dog. I met him when I picked you up freshman year, when we went to that band concert."

"How can you remember?" asked Gabriela.

"How can you *forget*?" Finn teased her. "You're the reason I took Spanish, you know."

Gabriela smiled.

"How is Algodón?" Finn asked.

"Someone ran over him. Didn't even pick him up off the street."

"That's tough," said Finn. "Scraps is dying. Bad tumors all over." Finn finished his pork tamal and began to unwrap his beef.

"Your father could help my family," Gabriela whispered.

Finn put down his fork.

"He came to our house the other day," Gabriela said. "To tell us he was selling. My father wants to buy the house, but he has no money. He asked your father to sell it over time, with no down payment." She drank the rest of her water.

"Doesn't sound like something Caldwell Dunmore would do," said Finn.

"My father blew up at him. He explodes about everything. I think it's because of me." Gabriela's eyes teared up. "To him, I'm nothing but a whore."

"*Una puta*," said Finn. "Parents." He shook his head.

"Maybe you could talk to your father? Help convince him about the house?"

"I guess I'll see him at the winter band concert."

"You guess?" Gabriela scooted her chair from the table and went to the bathroom.

Finn finished his beef tamal, then drank his water.

Gabriela stayed away a long time. When she returned, her eyes were swollen from her tears. "I must get home," said Gabriela. "My father, when he's gone, he calls sometimes, to make sure I'm there."

"I'll get you a doggie bag."

"No," said Gabriela. "I will take it to *el ciego*."

"*El ciego?*"

She nodded to the corner. "The blind one. Rosario's father. But he has a different kind of sight." She picked up her dessert tamal and took it to a small table by the cash register. Juan sat there most days, listening to the radio, smiling when someone called his name. Gabriela put the tamales on his plate and whispered something in his ear.

A smile creased the old man's face, and he nodded. When Gabriela started away, he called to her. She returned. He reached out his hand and touched her swollen belly as though he could see. "*Pronto*," he said, "*otro bebé* in the world. Mouth to smile, legs to run, mind to think. The world waits."

"*Yo también,*" said Gabriela.

Finn wished students could actually learn a foreign language in high school classes—not just study one. "*El ciego,*" he said when Gabriela came back to the table.

"Take this one for your dog." Gabriela wrapped half a chicken tamal in her napkin and handed it to him.

"Every dog in Topeka is going to follow me home." He left a twenty-dollar bill on the table.

Gabriela patted the blind man's hand on the way out. "*Gracias,* Juan." She waved to Rosaria.

"*Cuidado, hija,*" said the restaurant owner.

Finn and Gabriela walked the short way to her house. "I hope he hasn't called," she said.

Finn walked her up the sidewalk.

"Talk to your father?" Gabriela took Finn's hand and jumped over the missing stair onto the porch. She handed Finn his gloves and unlocked the door.

Finn walked home so he could feed Scraps. He unlocked the front door and pushed his way inside.

"Finn?" His mother's voice came from the dining room.

Carol sat at the table. All the boxes she'd brought down from the attic were open. Holiday decorations cluttered every surface. She was dwarfed by the stacks of accumulated Christmases. "What are you doing home on a Monday?" Finn asked.

"That's my question for you," she said.

"Brought home some lunch. For Scraps. You?"

"Trying to figure out Christmas. I want to get the tree up this week." She stood up. "I can't find the tree stand."

Finn dug in his jacket for the tamales. "I'll look for the stand later. Gotta get back to school. What's for dinner tonight?"

"Leftovers," said Carol.

In the back pantry Scraps lifted his thin head. Even two or

three months before, Scraps would have sniffed out the tamales in Finn's hands, would have been all legs and tongue. Half blind, Scraps leaned toward the tamal that Finn set in the bowl next to an untouched treat.

Carol came to stand behind him. She touched the back of his head. "Leftovers?" she asked.

"It's what he likes best." Finn stood up. "You didn't go to work? To study the old punctuation?"

"I went to Laurence's. After that, I needed to just come home and have some time."

"You okay?" he asked.

She nodded. "Let's buy a tree today," she said. "The Optimist lot still has some really big ones. I want a tree that will take up the whole house."

"I better get back to school," said Finn.

Carol stuck her nose in the air and sniffed, as though imitating what Scraps would have done the year before. "Rosaria's tamales? How did you have time for that?"

"I'm a good student. I'm going to graduate. They give me space," said Finn.

"Don't take advantage of them," said Carol.

Finn knew he should hurry back to school and play his trumpet. If he didn't skip band, or jazz band, or rehearsals, he was okay. And they were "deep in rehearsal," as Mr. Riley liked to say. Scraps whined, then whimpered as Finn left through the back door.

thursday, december 18

Tuesday and Wednesday of that week Carol found large envelopes from Laurence in the mail. Inside, no message. Just browning petals collected as the roses drooped, wilted, then let their petals go. Was he feeling so sorry for himself that he hadn't even put them in vases? Carol imagined Laurence bending laboriously in his chair, sweeping petals off tabletops, picking them up from the floor, his heart wilting as she refused to call, to acknowledge his challenge and his promise of change. She seemed as determined to ignore him as Finn was determined to ignore her desire to make a memorable Christmas together.

Carol continued her study of transitions; subtle changes, she noticed, were too often ignored. She read about London during Dickens' time, how suddenly this teeming, industrial city had real problems. The city was a stinking mess, the Thames draining raw sewage, the stink so horrid that people wore handkerchiefs over their faces, the dead lying in the streets in such numbers that those making a profit from such squalid conditions had to step over them and were finally forced to carry the stench, on their own boots, into their fine homes along with the smoke and pestilence that came into their lungs with each breath. Then, and only then, did the prominent of London improve conditions—after thousands and thousands of lesser canaries had died in the warehouses, the factories, the pestiferous streets. *Ah*, thought Carol, *transitions come hard: for Finn, for Laurence, even for herself.*

She was surprised, then, when Laurence called her first thing Thursday morning. "Your Mrs. Cross," he said. "She's wonderful. You must meet her tonight. For the Cratchit meal. Bring Finn."

Carol did not know what to say. She had hoped to distance herself from Laurence, but she hadn't yet found time for the tradition of her Cratchit meal, either.

"Carol, please. My goose may be cooked with you, but that doesn't mean I can't cook you a goose."

"Can we bring anything?"

"Gin and lemon, for after the pudding," he said. "Six o'clock."

Carol agreed. She hung up and went to her study carrel to count punctuation marks. She began with the semicolons in the Cratchit scene; the large number satisfied her. As did the invitation itself. For Laurence had been the reason Dickens was such a big part of her Christmas tradition.

Laurence Timmons had been her supervisor for years, and, after Caldwell left her, he had sent a Christmas card well before Thanksgiving. The card pictured a giant of a man, garlanded in greenery, surrounded by food, illustrating a quote from Dickens' *A Christmas Carol*:

have always thought of Christmas . . . as a good time; a
kind, forgiving, charitable, pleasant time: the only time I

know of, in the long calendar of the year, when men and women seem by one consent to open their shut-up hearts freely, and to think of people below them as if they really were fellow-passengers to the grave.

Inside Laurence had outlined his plan. He was supposed to attend a library meeting in London but wanted Carol to go in his place. If she could afford Finn's ticket, the library would take care of their lodging and her meals. Laurence would dog-sit Scraps.

Even though the wound of their separation was not nearly healed, Caldwell had offered to buy Finn's ticket as a Christmas gift when Carol told him about Laurence's plan, even though he wondered if the trip would be wasted on a ten-year-old. "And don't worry," Caldwell said to Finn. "When you get back, we'll have a real Christmas up in the loft. That is, if you don't freeze to death in London."

"It'll be warmer there than here," said Carol. "The foggy, snowy Christmas of Dickens' *A Christmas Carol* was inspired by an anomaly."

Later, Carol explained to Finn that their trip itself was an anomaly—something different, out of the ordinary, a once-in-a-lifetime unexpected occurrence. She made reservations at a bed-and-breakfast and planned an itinerary that would focus on Charles Dickens, at least until she had to satisfy her obligations at the library conference.

Though jet-lagged, she plunged them eagerly into London. They found a few pubs where Dickens had sat with friends, even sometimes written his work. They walked past the Athenaeum on Pall Mall, a club Dickens frequented. They found the intersection of Marylebone and Marylebone High Street and studied the stone bas-relief on a building there, placed in honor of

Dickens' residence at the site; there, he'd written six of his novels, including *A Christmas Carol*. Finn recognized Scrooge and the door knocker with Marley's face, if nothing else. They found the Dickens House Museum, on Doughty Street, and climbed up and down the stairs, from the library in the basement to the special exhibit on the third floor.

"Charles Dickens walked these same streets, these same paths, through these same gardens," said their tour guide the next day. She was costumed as Mrs. Cratchit. "Dressed out but poorly in a twice-turned gown," she said. "Of course, everything has changed. London is naught but change."

Carol found it hard to imagine Dickens or any of his characters—nephew Fred, Cratchit, Tiny Tim, Fezziwig—walking where she and Finn walked. Still, she dragged Finn along as she combed her guidebook in search of Dickens' life, his books, his Christmas. One afternoon she armed herself with a pocket street guide and a literary London book that promised a self-guided Dickens' London walk. They set off into the misty air. Streets changed names with each step they took. A single street might trick them, suddenly veering to become a Court, a Place, a Square, a Close, a Mews. They spent half their time ducking into storefronts to consult *London A–Z*. When they finally reached somewhere mentioned in the guidebook, like as not the place wasn't real: it had *once* been the home of London's poorest, or London's Italian Quarter, or the site of a prison, tavern, or tenement in which one of Dickens' characters—Oliver Twist, say—had joined with Fagin, who was named, according to the book, after a young man Dickens had worked with during the humiliation of his youthful employment in the blacking factory. Of course, almost everything had *once* been and did not exist now. The Italian Quarter was nothing but low-slung warehouses. The Holborn Hill of *Oliver*

Twist had been torn down to make Holborn Viaduct. The site of Newgate prison was now the site of the Central Criminal Court, Old Bailey. Carol pointed out the clock on St. Andrew's Church at Holborn Circus, mentioned by Dickens in *Oliver Twist*.

"I'm thirsty," Finn said.

"You're a dear," said Carol. "I'm suddenly pooped."

They found a pub, dark inside, with intricately cut wood from floor to vaulted ceiling. They sat in a booth opposite a big box that was a wood-burning stove. Finn craned his neck, reading the signs for beers, brews, ales, stouts, and lagers, for biscuits and cigarettes and teas. "Did Charles Dickens ever come in here?" Finn asked.

Carol erupted, laughing so hard she began to cry. She held a handkerchief to her face. After a minute she composed herself. "Dickens, here?" she said. "Probably. Wasn't he everywhere?" She tried to smile. "And isn't he exactly nowhere?" She pointed to her guidebook. "Dickens' London is gone. Replaced by roads and viaducts and modern buildings. Ugly ones, at that. You saw those monstrosities obscuring St. Paul's. My God." She put her head in her hands. "I don't know if Laurence sent me here to discover Dickens, or to discover Dickens' absence."

"You keep telling me we're walking where Dickens walked," Finn reminded her.

"And where thousands of other people walked. George Orwell, and Charles Darwin, and Emmeline Pankhurst—the British suffragist—and now Finn Dickens-Dunmore. Now that you've walked here, we can go home."

"Are we going to read *A Christmas Carol* like you promised?"

"I don't know," said Carol. She finished her tea. She stood up and dumped the guidebook into her purse.

"You promised," said Finn.

"I have to prepare for the conference."

"You're bad," said Finn.

"I'm *not* bad, I just *feel* bad," said Carol. "I expected at least a *little* bit more of the trappings of Charles Dickens and *A Christmas Carol.*"

"I didn't expect anything," said Finn. "But I know where *Christmas Carol* is. It's back at the hotel. And we're reading it."

"Maybe," said Carol. "Now come on."

Finn refused to move. "Do you remember the Grinch?" he whispered, so Carol bent down to hear him. "And when he stole Christmas it didn't matter to the Whos, right? Remember how they sang anyway?"

"Of course."

"You're a Bad Who," said Finn. "You're just a Bad Old Who."

"You're right." Carol shook her head. "I wish I had Christmas in my heart. Like those Whos. I really wish I did."

"They're just words on a page," said Finn, speaking like his teachers might, like Carol might. "And all you have to do is read those words."

Carol sat back down. "I will," she said.

She started *A Christmas Carol* with Finn that very night and continued through the next, and the next, finishing on Christmas Day. Dickens' London was in every word, unerasable. And like Good Whos, she and Finn made Christmas under a small tree in the pinched sitting room of their bed-and-breakfast. He gave her a souvenir map of Dickens' London he'd found at the Dickens House. She gave him three novels about boys: *Oliver Twist*, *David Copperfield*, and *Great Expectations*. "You're not too young to read them," Carol told him. "You're a big boy. And smart. And a great London companion."

Now, the little boy, the great companion of that trip, was a head taller than she was and still just as stubborn to have his way. Smart, yes. But leaving in less than a month; in fact, he was *already* leaving, she discovered, when she went to the mailbox. Besides another envelope from Laurence, filled with rose petals, she found a note from Mr. Riley, the Topeka High band director, who wrote that Finn had been faithful to his music classes, and to band rehearsals, but other teachers had expressed concern at Finn's absences from their classes. "You know," he wrote, "that I have the utmost respect for Finn, and he has been the mainstay of what has been an excellent trumpet section and band. In fact, I regret his leaving, since spring is so stacked with the usual competitions where Finn excels. But other teachers may report him to those higher up in the chain of command, those who do not have the forbearance that I will always have for Finn, given his usual loyalty and fine musicianship." He asked if Finn had special circumstances he should report, and would she please talk to Finn and call him?

Right after school, his backpack slung over his shoulder, his trumpet case in hand, Finn trudged in a light snow through downtown and across the Kansas Avenue Bridge into North Topeka. He imagined his mother sitting in the darkening house, her eyes still wrinkled from squinting over her books, counting punctuation. For the past four days he had eaten lunch at Rosaria's with Gabriela. Then he'd walked home to feed Scraps their leftover chicken tamales, then returned to school. Senior year everything loosened up. Finn blessed his free periods, his study halls and independent studies, with teachers who knew how to cut good students a little slack. Finn blessed administrators too busy with the "problem kids" to worry about the couple of hours Finn stole from the middle of the day. Most of all, Finn blessed Gabriela. She understood him when he talked: about his needy mother, his long-absent father, his few teachers who couldn't see he was already out of there, his plans for himself once he was away at college, how he wanted to understand music like he'd never had time to, see it differently from anyone else in the world. She understood his love for Scraps, his ability to care when most kids were too cool to give a damn. Gabriela laughed at him when he stuttered in Spanish, but he could tell she liked him to try. She liked him to worry about her.

She asked each day if he had talked to his father. Finn wanted to wait for the end of the semester concerts, where he'd see his father anyway, but Gabriela was urgent. A new owner might kick them out or raise the rent. They might even have to go back to Mexico, her father had said, now that she had shamed the family.

"But maybe the house won't sell for a while," Gabriela said. "And in less than two weeks, it won't matter."

"Why?" asked Finn.

"I'll be eighteen," Gabriela said. "My father will have no control over me. I will move out of the house."

"Until then?" Finn asked.

"I pray he doesn't do something crazy. Until then, the little one must wait." She patted her womb.

"I don't understand," said Finn.

"Before I'm eighteen, my father can decide what happens to my baby. He will force me to give it to another family. After my birthday, I can decide."

"What will *you* decide?" asked Finn.

"I don't have to know until December twenty-ninth," said Gabriela.

"How can I help you?" asked Finn.

"Already you are helping me," said Gabriela.

On Tuesday, Finn had run from Topeka High School into Oakland to arrive at Rosaria's first, wait in line, and secure a table. Gabriela came in from the cold and found him. A woman approached their table. "You come in and you don't sit with me?" she asked Gabriela.

"I didn't see you, Tía," said Gabriela.

"You have eyes for someone else?" Gabriela's aunt stared down at Finn.

Finn stood up and reached out his hand. "I'm Finn Dickens-Dunmore," he said. "A friend from school. From band."

"I am Teresa, Gabriela's aunt." The woman took Finn's hand, appraising him. "What do you play in the band, Finn? Are you yet another drummer?" Gabriela's aunt rolled her dark eyes and crossed her arms over her chest.

"Trumpet," he said.

"I hope you play better than our Gabriela," said Teresa. "She was playing with us. In our mariachi band."

"I was trying," said Gabriela.

"And then you see what happened," said her aunt. "*Embarazada*. Pregnant."

Finn sat down. "*Mucho gusto*," he said. "Nice to meet you."

Teresa started away, then came back. "Maybe you'd like to listen? See if you like the music? We rehearse today at four thirty. Then again on Thursday. Gabriela knows where. I'll tell her father she needs to come again. She'll tell you how to find us. Bring your horn."

Finn shrugged, but Gabriela nodded yes. After Tía Teresa left, Finn leaned close to Gabriela. "Will your father let you come to the rehearsal?"

"Teresa is my *mother's* sister," said Gabriela. "He doesn't dare cross her."

So that Tuesday Finn hurried from school to North Topeka.

He listened to the band for a half hour, then took out his trumpet. "We have only a few pieces of music for you to read," said Teresa. "The traditional music, we older ones have it in here, and here." She put her hand to her head, then over her heart. "When there is no music, find what is in your heart. Improvise." Finn did his best and promised to return.

Now Finn was keeping his promise, trudging through Topeka on a cold Thursday, the middle three fingers of his right hand lifting off the handle of his trumpet case in rhythm to music that had already begun to live in his head. He liked the wailing, the staccato syncopations, the close harmonies of the sometimes boisterous, sometimes plaintive, music from Mexico. Of course, he'd known about mariachi all his life, starting with his family's annual pilgrimages to the Mexican Fiesta held each July during what always seemed the hottest days imaginable. He'd noticed the costumes first: the wide-brimmed hats, the spangled shirts and pants, the colorful swaths of cloth the same red and green as the Mexican flag. Then he noticed the instrumentation: violins, guitars—from small to the big *guitarrón*—and trumpets. When he heard the music, he imagined playing it just as Folklórica played each year, as did other mariachi bands from Texas and Mexico during the weeklong fiesta that raised funds for the Guadalupe school.

Finn knocked on the storefront door and boot steps clattered down the stairs with an "*Un momento.*" A fourteen-year-old trumpeter opened the door and smiled a greeting. "Our gringo," said the boy, smiling.

"El Señor Gringo, *joven*," said Finn.

Up the stairs and in what had once been a ballroom, the band members were tuning their instruments, strumming and sawing, banging and adjusting. Gabriela sat along the wall. With her was the old woman Finn had seen the first time he walked past Gabriela's house. The woman sat with her arms folded over her chest. Finn went straight to her and held out his hand, but the woman did not take it. "So you are the young man?" she asked.

Gabriela elbowed her. "Abuela," she whispered harshly, *"un amigo, sólo, no más."*

"What are you doing here?" the old woman asked Finn. She adjusted a shawl over long white hair.

"I came to play my trumpet." He lifted the trumpet case.

"And my Gabriela must be here for you to play?"

Finn hoisted his trumpet case onto a chair and unlatched it. His lips would serve him better on the horn than they would trying to form words. Let the old woman think what she wanted to think. Adults were always laying their ideas, their hang-ups, their craziness, on their children and grandchildren. Finn liked Gabriela. He wanted to help her. Finn liked the music. Finn didn't want to be at home or at school. Everything should just be simple, he wanted to tell Gabriela's *abuela*. He supposed they all thought he had something to do with Gabriela's pregnancy.

He blew into his horn, climbed up and down his range, puckered his lips, smiled at the old woman. Then he didn't think about anything but the music, its sonorous lamenting, its barking joy, its whooping pleasure in the rises and falls, its intricate rhythms. When he had no music to read, when none of them looked at notes, he listened to the other trumpeter. The horns were often punctuation, as his mother might say, to the music: exclamation points, quick question marks with even quicker answers, underlinings, stuttering commas and transitional dashes and semicolons. He wasn't the music, but he helped the music be what it was. In band he was used to melody, to playing the whole sentence. He enjoyed being the punctuation.

After a short hour, he shook hands with Gabriela and offered his hand to her *abuela*. The old woman touched his hand lightly. Finn started home in increasing snow. By the time he reached the Topeka Avenue Bridge, his footprints were crunching into an inch of slush, and his hair and eyelashes were crusted with large wet flakes. He stopped to put his hood up and his gloves on. A familiar truck pulled to the curb next to him and the door swung open. "Hop in," said Mr. Marble. A car honked behind the truck.

Finn hurried into the seat and swung the door shut as Mr. Marble stepped on the gas and started over the bridge.

"Your mother awaits," said Mr. Marble.

"My mother sent you?" Finn looked out the window, at the twilight snow, at the slushy river with its darkening sandbars, at the Union Pacific tracks, a slow train of coal cars snaking its way through a curve before heading west on what would be nothing but straightaway.

Mr. Marble was silent.

"She knows where I am?" Finn asked.

"Nobody knows where you are except for you," said Mr. Marble.

Finn smiled. Such was Mr. Marble. Enigmatic, maybe even a little crazy. "How's the chimney business?" asked Finn.

"Never been better. Got a special contract," said Mr. Marble. "Santa Claus himself. Tired of all the dirty chimneys, he is. So, I'm busy."

"Must be hard in this weather," said Finn.

"Hard time of year," said Mr. Marble. "Take your mother. She's feeling it, isn't she?"

"Feeling what?"

"The dark. The cold. The loneliness when people aren't there for her."

"Did she talk to you or something?" asked Finn.

"I hear things, I do," said Mr. Marble. "I'm a chimney sweep. I have an ear for what's going on up and down the rooftops and the chimneys that connect the roofs to the rooms, and to the hearts of those inside them."

Mr. Marble turned down Third Street, his back tires sliding enough that Finn grabbed the door. Then Marble turned onto Finn's street and crept to a stop. "And don't worry about your Gabriela," said Mr. Marble. "She and her family will be fine."

"What?" asked Finn.

"Take care of your mother," Mr. Marble said. He revved the engine and Finn hopped out. "Later or sooner." The old man waved, and off he drove, the passenger door still half open.

Finn's house was completely dark.

Carol called Laurence to decline his invitation to the Cratchit meal, explaining her circumstances with Finn. Laurence protested, hoping she jested, just as Cratchit's family tried to fool Bob by telling him that Martha would not be coming to the family dinner. "Be like Martha," he said. "Pop out of the door so that I might not be disappointed."

"I wish I could," said Carol. She hung up.

She regretted missing the tradition, the chance to meet Mrs. Cross in person, perhaps hear another promise from Laurence. Regret fueled her disappointment in Finn. Then she turned to herself. Hadn't she noticed uneaten tamales gathering in Scraps' bowl? Hadn't she tolerated Finn's long silences at the dinner table? Hadn't she been unsure of herself this Christmas, wanting her traditions, but not forcing them? Not forcing anything—responsibility, duty, conversation?

When the door opened, she snapped on the lamp next to her chair. "You had to stay after school?" she asked a soggy Finn.

"Is it late?" he asked.

"Not too late to tell me what's going on with you," said Carol. She held up Mr. Riley's note. Then she lifted her other hand, with another letter. "After you read what your band director has to say, why don't you read your father's latest."

Finn took the pieces of paper. He turned on the overhead light and sat on the couch. Scraps moaned from the pantry to acknowledge Finn's arrival. When Finn finished Mr. Riley's letter, he turned to his father's. Once he'd read them, he threw them both on the coffee table.

"I can explain," he said. "About lunch, and after school." He folded his arms and leaned back against the cushions.

"So explain," said Carol. She was tempted to stand up, cross her arms, tower over him as she did when he was a child. But he might just stand up.

"I've been helping a friend. Having lunch with her. Talking." He put his feet on the coffee table. "They don't need me at school. I've been skipping part of the day. But nobody really cares. Mr. Riley's just nervous about the concerts, like usual."

"Your feet are wet," Carol said. She moved forward in her chair and Finn sat up straight. He took off his shoes. "And after school?" Carol asked.

"At Rosaria's I met this woman who has the mariachi band. She asked me to sit in. That's where I was. Playing the trumpet. Mr. Riley makes us play the same thing over and over. I know the music. I knew it by heart after a week of rehearsal." He stood up. "God, Mom, I'm just trying to learn something new. Why do you think I'm graduating early? Why do you think I'm getting out of here?" He walked to his backpack and his trumpet.

"You are staying home tonight," said Carol. "In your room. No walking."

"Walking?"

"I know you're out some nights. I've trusted you. Until now."

"I'm not doing anything wrong," Finn insisted.

"I believe that. I want to, anyway. Tomorrow you will talk to your teachers first thing. You will apologize. And you will not skip classes. Is that clear?"

Finn nodded his head.

"Look at me," she said. "Is that clear?"

"Yes," he said, meeting her eyes.

"And tomorrow, after school, you will come straight home. Is that clear?"

Finn nodded again.

"Do I have to tell you to look at me?" Carol said.

"Why did you want me to read Dad's letter?" he asked, staring her down. "Is that why you've been on my case? Because you can't be on his?"

Carol sighed. She shouldn't have pushed this business onto her son. Had Caldwell already talked to him about the move? Maybe they'd both had plans to leave long before she learned about either Finn's college applications or Caldwell's new business venture. "Do you remember the Christmas your father left?" asked Carol.

Finn sat on the couch. "You broke every single ornament in the house," he said.

"I stomped on the glass balls, I crushed the ceramic pieces, I ripped paper, and I cut fabric. I didn't care if they were pigs, chile peppers, cats, lambs, or the baby Jesus. I only saved the ones I'd picked out. And then I sat on the couch where you're sitting now. And I cried." Carol leaned forward in her chair. "I didn't cry because of the destruction. I was still angry. I cried because once I destroyed everything, I saw how little of myself had ever been on those trees. Seven St. Nicholases. A half dozen Victorian carolers. All men."

"I'm a man," said Finn.

"Oh, honey, I'm not mad at you. I'm just trying to tell you how I feel. Your father left us a long time ago. I'm not angry about his leaving again. But I'm having a hard time, it's true."

"We still decorated a tree that year," Finn reminded her.

They had indeed. Carol had cut thin apple slices, against the core, so each round slice, dried in a slow oven, revealed a star. She took needle and thread and strung the Christmas cards they'd received. She and Finn made strings of popcorn and cranberries. They glued strips of construction paper into loops that went through loops, until chains of bright paper festooned the branches of the Douglas fir. Carol brought down her costume jewelry and hung earrings, bracelets, and necklaces. Finn added his two neckties. His Lego men found themselves secured to thin boughs. By the end of the evening, Carol and Finn's tree bulged, glittered, and glowed in a resplendence of colors and good intentions.

"Can we start all over again?" asked Carol.

"What do you mean?"

"Tomorrow, after school. We'll go for a Christmas tree."

"I found the tree stand," he said. "In the carriage house." Finn smiled as he grabbed his things and went upstairs.

Carol went to fix dinner. Not a Cratchit dinner, but homely fare for a night when she had wished for more. As she prepared a ham steak, rice, and canned corn—no cornucopia this night— she thought of her first Cratchit meal, the December after Caldwell left.

She and Finn had gone to the university library. Charles Dickens' great-grandson Cedric, it turned out, had published *Dining with Dickens*, with an entire chapter on Christmas. For backup Carol found Eliza Acton's *Modern Cookery for Private*

Families, an 1845 compendium of how nineteenth-century English people cooked and ate. The recipes were called "receipts." How often Carol had been admonished by Caldwell to "keep your receipts." *Screw Caldwell*, she had thought. She kept her own kind of receipts, the ones for food, not income taxes.

"Screw Caldwell," her friend Freda had echoed. "Christmas is for merriment, not for humbugs like your soon-to-be ex." With Freda, everything was "soon-to-be." Carol was soon-to-be fully divorced, soon-to-be happy, soon-to-be finding her own rituals, soon-to-be learning more about herself, exploring her own tastes, adjusting to single life and single motherhood.

Freda and Carol shopped together and bought one small goose, two large potatoes, two apples to cook down to sauce, one onion and a loaf of bread for stuffing, one apple, one orange, and a dozen chestnuts. The basic meal was simple enough, but not the pudding. Cedric Dickens' simple receipt called for bread crumbs and brown sugar. Orange and lemon peel. Spice, eggs, salt. Freda ran to the liquor store for rum and Guinness while Carol asked the butcher for suet. He seemed amused that she might actually use it for cooking and gave it to her free. Carol searched for currants and sultanas and muscatels: three different names for grapes, as she'd found out. Currants were the small Mediterranean seedless; sultanas, the seedless Asia Minor golden; muscatels, the raisin of the sweet white muscat grape. All those grapes. No wonder the pudding was the centerpiece of the Christmas feast: bread and grapes, the same ingredients as communion, only the bread crumbed and sweetened, the grapes dried instead of fermented.

She and Freda had gone home to assemble the pudding, which sang in its steam for five hours. Carol felt the same anxiety as Mrs. Cratchit upon turning it out. And had the same rich reward, and, as Dickens wrote, she entered the dining room "flushed, but smiling proudly—with the pudding, like a speckled cannon-ball, so hard and firm, blazing in half of half-a-quartern of ignited brandy, and bedight with Christmas holly stuck into the top. Oh, a wonderful pudding!"

"Soon-to-be eaten!" Freda exclaimed.

Finn refused to eat it. Freda ate generously, especially the outer layer, immersed as it was in brandy. Carol ate a healthy portion, then cleared the pudding from the table. She did not let Finn's grumpiness affect her. Not this, her first Christmas after the separation, a Christmas "brave in ribbons," as Dickens had written, when life was in tatters. Carol served the apple and orange, the roasted chestnuts, which she helped Finn peel—and still he ate only a bite. She and Freda lifted their small toddies of gin and lemon, and Carol forced herself to say, "A Merry Christmas to us all. God bless us!"

Finn refused to say "God bless us everyone," though Carol had rehearsed him.

Freda chimed in with the obligatory line, standing in her red blouse and long green skirt, her wool socks and sandals indicating her past as a flower child. Carol wondered how she'd have weathered the season without her friend. Carol blessed Scraps with the skin of the goose.

The next day Carol had given the leftover pudding to Mr. Marble, who had come for a ladder from the carriage house. He hefted the foil, then brought it to his nose. "A Christmas pudding, you say," the old had man said. "Right heavy enough. And with the proper smell of a drunkard's breath."

Now, the Cratchit meal missed, Carol could still become whatever she was soon-to-be.

The Cratchit Meal

Menu

Small Goose with Sage and Onion

INGREDIENTS
Goose, 8 to 10 lbs.
Salt, to rub skin
Butter, 1 tbsp.

Sage and Onion

Sage, leaves, ½ oz., minced
Onions, 2 medium, parboiled and chopped finely
Salt, 1 tsp.
Pepper, ½ tsp.
Butter, 1 tbsp.

Mix sage and onion together with spices and butter and place inside bird. Smear bottom of roasting pan with butter and rub salt over skin of trussed goose. Put in 350-degree oven and bake for about 20 minutes per pound (3½ hours for a 10-pound goose). Drain fat occasionally. Carve at the table.

Applesauce

INGREDIENTS
Apples, about 1 lb., any kind, according to taste
Water, 1 or 2 tbsp.
Butter, 1 tbsp., optional
Sugar, 1 tbsp., optional
Lemon, small amount of rind
Pepper, several dashes

Peel and core apples into cold water for freshness, put in saucepan with water, and cook on low heat until apple is soft. Sauce it with remaining ingredients.

Mashed Potatoes

Potatoes, Russet, ⅔ a potato per person
Butter, 1 tbsp. per each two potatoes
Salt, ½ tsp.
Milk, ¼ cup

Scrub the potatoes, but do not peel or remove eyes, and, starting with cold water, bring to a boil, then simmer until done. Pour off water and let steam evaporate, then remove skins and mash with salt, butter, and milk (or cream if you're not a Cratchit). Sprinkle with pepper and serve hot.

Pudding

Bread, crumbed, 7 oz.
Flour, 7 oz.
Currants, 12 oz.
Raisins, 12 oz.
Sugar, 6 oz.
Candied peel, mixed, 3 oz.
Lemon, rind of 1
Nutmeg, ½ tsp. ground
Mixed spice, ½ tsp.
Salt, pinch or more
Suet, 8 oz.
Eggs, 4 medium, whisked
Brandy, 4 oz.

Mix bread, flour, currants, raisins, sugar, and spices with the suet until blended. Add eggs and brandy, moisten well, and leave in bowl until next day. Then place in cloth and steam for at least 5 hours.

Roasted Chestnuts

Chestnuts, 6 per person
Salt, for the table

Cut the rind of each nut slightly. Boil for 7 to 10 minutes and then dry. Put them in an oven at 350 degrees for 15 minutes. Serve hot, seasoning them with salt at the table.

Apples, ½ per person, sliced
Oranges, ½ per person, sliced

Gin and Lemon

INGREDIENTS
Gin, ½ pint
Water, ½ pint
Lemon, 1 sliced thinly
Sugar, ¼ cup

Mix water, gin, sugar, and lemons in small saucepan and barely heat (you don't want to lose the alcohol) until ready to serve with chestnuts and apple and orange slices.

friday, december 19

After a day with punctuation, made more pleasurable by the prospect of a Christmas tree, Carol eagerly approached the mailbox. But Laurence missed a day of petals. She was unexpectedly hurt by their absence. The sky darkened. She unlocked the house and went to the pantry to greet Scraps. Finn had not been home, or at least not left the usual tamales in the dog's bowl. She shook a dog treat from the box. Scraps ignored it. The two of them moped, then perked up when Finn opened the door. Scraps whined. Carol bustled down the hall toward him. "Don't take off your coat. Don't kick off your shoes. We're off for the tree."

"I'm hungry," said Finn.

"We'll grab something when we're out," said Carol.

"What about Scraps?" Finn asked.

"He has a treat, but not much interest in it," said Carol. "Go give him a hug."

Finn didn't move.

"Give him a hug and let's go. Unless you want to sit down

with me in the living room and discuss your day in detail. Your talk with your teachers? Or we could talk about your father."

"I'll go, I'll go," said Finn.

After the Scraps check and the locking of the house, they headed toward the Optimist lot. Carol knew the fullest tree, the one she'd coveted, had already been sold. But they could still find a suitable tree. It was only the nineteenth of December. Lots of people waited until their kids were out of school. Some still did what her father used to do—put up the tree as a surprise at the very last minute.

"You been talking to Dad?" Finn asked. "Have you made any decisions?"

"Not yet," said Carol. She drove in silence until they turned into the Optimist lot. "Pick out a tree. Your choice." She opened her door and walked past the little trailer where two men sat smoking cigarettes and watching television. One of them waved. Finn remained in the Subaru. Carol sized up Blue spruce, Douglas fir, and Scotch pine, all compacted from being wrapped tightly for shipment. She found several that might fill their living room. She knew the firs would smell richest, bringing the season to their noses as well as their eyes. Carol went behind a row of trees to wait out Finn's resistance. A wet snow stopped falling. The clouds moved slowly away, stars twinkling between puffs and billows. A clear night would mean real cold. After a few minutes, Carol couldn't help but pull a tree from where it leaned against the makeshift fence. Though it was half again her height, she held it at arm's length, like a large dance partner, turning it so she could judge it from all sides. She nodded approvingly. One of the Optimists approached her. "You found yourself the best tree on the lot," he said.

"I always do," said Carol.

"But your young fella found what he wants. He said you'd

pay." The man pulled a pack of cigarettes from his jacket pocket and tamped one out. "Your son?" he asked.

Carol nodded. "He's going to college next month."

The man lit his cigarette, took a deep drag, and blew the smoke into the sky. "I'm not going to charge you anything for the tree he picked out. You can tell him you paid me back here. Or I can tell him the tree's not for sale."

"That bad?" Carol smiled.

"Once I took my little girl to the pound. She picked the mangiest, skinniest, raggedy kitten. But she loved it dearly. She's off to college herself. I swear she misses that cat more'n she misses me."

"But not more than you miss her?" asked Carol.

The man busied himself with his cigarette. Carol walked from behind the rows of trees toward the little trailer. Finn's spruce didn't even reach his shoulders. When he spun it for her, she could see the gaps, the mismatched lengths of the branches, the total lack of symmetry, the bunch of needles huddled together near the middle. The Optimist was right: he had picked the worst tree on the lot. The other man came out of the trailer and dutifully cut an inch from the bottom of the tree trunk. "So it's even shorter," Carol said. "I've already paid," Carol said to Finn. "Let's go make a home for your tree." She reached into her purse and threw Finn the keys. He opened the back of the wagon. For once the tree fit in easily, no moving the back seat forward, no twining the rear hatch to the bumper because the bottom of a huge tree jutted out.

Finn hurried to the passenger seat and climbed in. Carol waved a thanks to the man in the lot. When she opened her door, Finn asked, "Did you see what was in the tree?"

"*In* the tree?" asked Carol.

"You don't know everything," said Finn.

They picked up Chinese at their favorite restaurant—Chow Fun Singapore Style for Finn, Curry Shrimp for Carol. They went to the liquor store for Carol's favorite seasonal beer—Boulevard's Nutcracker Ale. At the video store, they rented *It's a Wonderful Life*. All through their errands Finn refused to tell her what was in the tree.

Finn carried the tree into the house. Carol carried the tree stand into the hallway and held the miserable little nothing of a tree in the base of the stand while Finn twisted the screws into the trunk. The tree listed slightly, but Carol didn't insist on perfection. Anything right about the tree's position in the stand would just call attention to all that was wrong with the tree. And so much *was* wrong.

Except that just above where she held the trunk of the tree, where the branches seemed clumped together, Carol saw what Finn had seen. She pulled out the bird's nest, woven expertly from needles, straw, leaves, string, feathers, even a length of what looked like green tooth floss—all mudded together to shape a rounded nest as elegant, as perfect, as the tree was pitiful. "Cool, huh?" asked Finn.

Carol sat down and held the nest in her lap. "Do you think I should stay in this house?" She pointed to the mantel, where she'd put Caldwell's letter. "You'd be more comfortable when you come home from college."

"Let's eat," said Finn. "Let's decorate this dumb little tree. Let's be Good Whos, and sing, and forget about the Grinch."

So they ate and decorated and sang and watched *It's a Wonderful Life*.

"We're a little behind, Finn," Carol said at the end of the evening. "But perhaps small and adequate will be our way of doing things this year. Like the Cratchit meal we skipped? But first, how about Christmas Past? Sunday? The Fezziwig meal?"

"Always planning the next thing," said Finn.

"You'd live without plans?"

"I'd just live," said Finn. They'd only used one string of lights for Finn's small tree. He picked up the bag with three more strings at the bottom. "I'm putting these up outside. Brighten things a little."

Carol watched him from the front window as he untangled the lights and strung them along the porch rail and up and down the posts that held up the porch roof. He created no pattern, no symmetry. When he came back inside, he asked for hot chocolate. Carol made a toddy—gin, butter, and lemon juice—for herself.

"Tomorrow," said Finn as they sat in the living room in the glow from the one string of lights, "I'm going to buy more lights. Get Mr. Marble to help me run them all the way up the chimney. And put a star on top."

Carol thought of Finn's room, the stars everywhere. From early on he'd patterned everything. Now he claimed to be "just living." Carol wondered if he was having as many problems as she was with what might come next.

"That'd be wonderful," she said. Caldwell's letter still rested on the mantelpiece. Carol drank the last of her toddy. "Everything is going to be fine."

After Carol came upstairs, Finn debated going out. The walk would be slushy and cold. He'd seen Gabriela already, at lunch. And his mother would be watching him closely. He tried to sleep, but couldn't. He lay in his bed and listened to the trains, their rumbling wheels, their plaintive whistles. He heard the occasional gust of winter wind in his chimney top. He heard the music, first band, then mariachi, the phrases repeating themselves, becoming part of his brain as most music did. He thought of Gabriela in her bed, in her room, in her house with the broken stair and the for sale sign, in her neighborhood of small houses, the same neighborhood where Rosaria cooked the best tamales in Topeka, where the basement of Our Lady of Guadalupe Church was full of the smells of the food the fiesta king and queen candidates sold in the months leading up to the Mexican Fiesta, the best time for mariachi, for the sounds of the music in his head. That music went out from the church and the neighborhood and played with the wind over all the city, until Finn imagined it waking up Mr. Riley, who lived miles away, out in the country on Carlson Road. The music would drift into the cracks in the band director's double-car garage and waft into his dreams, bringing color and an exotic pleasure the man might mistake for a subtle taste in his mouth, a soft touch on his skin, a new dream to replace the ones in which children marched in patterns on football fields. Finn had once heard that sound never dissipates but keeps traveling into the universe. He wondered at all the sounds he had made—where were they now?

Into his waking sleep, because he knew he had drifted off, came a guttural whine, soft and pleading. Only after Scraps called a second and a third time did Finn wake enough to clamber down the stairs. When Scraps saw Finn, he tried to lift his head off his bony paws. He whined again—sharper, clearer, more pitiful. Carol came downstairs. Scraps whined again, a high-pitched groan of pain, when he saw her. The food that mother and son had offered during the day lay untouched. The water bowl was empty, spilled. Scraps lay in the small puddle, his white and rust fur matted. When Finn tried to move Scraps, the dog nipped at his hand and growled. "We have to dry him off," Finn said.

Carol went for a towel. "Just try to get it under him," she said.

Finn did his best and Scraps quit snapping. The dog had been in such pain for so long, nearly uncomplaining. Carol and Finn's attention seemed to unleash weeks of repressed suffering. Scraps moaned, whined, groaned—all in an almost human voice—until tears welled in Finn's eyes.

"I'm calling Matt Groner," said Carol, and Finn nodded.

Scraps quieted. Finn lifted him onto the towel that soaked up the spilled water.

"He's coming over." Carol brought a blanket from the front closet, and the two of them laid it over Scraps. They sat on the floor quietly, ears cocked, listening for the sound of a car, for footsteps, for a knock on the door. "Do you know what Dr. Groner will probably say?" Carol asked Finn.

Finn nodded, but he held up his hand to stop Carol's voice. He wanted to sit and wait quietly, with no thought of the future.

Scraps' ears perked, and he made a satisfied groan in his throat. A minute later the doorbell rang, and Carol went to lead Matt Groner to the kitchen pantry. The veterinarian had a dark growth of beard stubble and sleep-spiked hair, but his eyes were the same steady blue Finn was used to. Dr. Groner put down his bag and kneeled next to Finn and Scraps.

"How's my old guy tonight?" Matt Groner spoke directly to Scraps, who whimpered.

"That bad?" asked the vet. He touched Scraps' head, just above the eyes, with both thumbs. When Scraps moaned, Matt Groner massaged up and down the long bone of the dog's nose. "A fever," he observed. "Dehydrated, too. Not a great situation for an old trooper like Scraps." Matt Groner patted Finn on the back, put his hand on Finn's head, and stood up. "If we were in the office I could do an IV. Antibiotic, fluids, the whole bit. For now, I'm going to give Scraps a shot. Simple pain relief. Morphine.

Scraps will sleep. When he wakes up, you'll bring him to the office. I'll teach you how to hydrate him."

"He doesn't like anybody to touch him," Finn said.

"We're going to have to think about what he needs, not what he likes," the vet said.

"Is it time?" asked Carol.

"Let's do an evaluation tomorrow. Or Monday," said Dr. Groner. "Finn," he said, and sat down on the floor. He put his hand on Finn's knee. "You're a fine fellow. You've done all you can. I know you have."

"Do you mean I've done the right stuff?" Finn asked. "Or do you mean there's nothing more I can do?"

"We'll find out tomorrow," said the vet. He went to his bag, found the syringe, and filled it from a small bottle. Scraps did not flinch when Dr. Groner put the needle into his thigh, but Finn and Carol did. Scraps closed his eyes almost immediately. "Let's all get some sleep now," said Matt Groner. "I'll let myself out."

stave three

plans

saturday, december 20

Carol woke up early to check on Scraps, who was still asleep, sighing more than breathing. Finn would sleep in. Carol braved her frozen driveway for the newspaper, double-wrapped in thin pink plastic and already soggy. She spread the paper on the dining table and found she'd opened it to a small article on Caldwell. First was the news that Caldwell Dunmore was selling his development business and decamping to Arizona. "To greener pastures," the paper reported. The paper quoted a real estate broker, who called Dunmore a "mover and a shaker. Nobody has *done more* for Topeka's downtown development." As in many Midwestern capitals, the central city had been decimated by mall development—first White Lakes Mall, then West Ridge, one named for a half a lake, the other for half a ridge. "Topeka should have *done more* to support Caldwell Dunmore," the paper wrote. "Everyone wishes him luck in his next endeavor."

Mover and shaker, indeed, thought Carol. The first time she'd read that in the Topeka paper, she'd called Laurence. "He did move out of your house. He did shake you and Finn up,"

Laurence had said. Carol glanced at Caldwell's letter. The day's mail might bring more petals. Or maybe Laurence would give up on her, as Caldwell had. Maybe that's what she deserved. But not what she wanted. Christmas would proceed with the Fezziwig feast. She would call Laurence; he'd be interested in Scraps' fate, if nothing else.

Finn tumbled down the stairs after ten o'clock. "Scraps is going to make it," she said. "At least through Christmas."

"Did Scraps reassure you, or are you reassuring me?" Finn frowned.

"I promise, Finn," Carol said. "Grab an apple and let's go."

They transferred Scraps to a long pillow and covered him with a blanket. Finn reached under the dog with both arms and forklifted Scraps straight up, keeping the pillow flat. Carol held the doors, and they put Scraps in the back of the Subaru wagon. Pine needles littered the floor; the faint smell of the tree still lingered.

Carol and Finn drove in silence. In her own way Carol prayed. Her friend Freda called it "meditating on single thoughts." Carol had done it since she was a child, as in "maybe Santa will bring me a pair of skates." Or as a teenager: "He will ask me out, I know he will." Or as an adult: "I will survive this, I will survive this." For Scraps, she thought, *After Christmas, please. Please let it be after Christmas.*

Matt Groner took over. Scraps seemed better than he expected. He wanted to keep the dog until Monday, with a weekend regimen of IV fluids, more pain killers, and then a thorough exam. "If he's doing better, I can teach you to hydrate him, and we'll go from there."

"If not?" Carol asked.

"I'll call you Monday."

Finn wanted to call Mr. Marble, then shop for the Christmas

lights they'd hang the next day. Carol dropped him off at home. He walked quickly up the sidewalk, lifting his legs high to keep his shoes from waterlogging in the slushy snow. He had always been such a determined walker. A determined boy. Had to be, she guessed. She shouldn't have been surprised when he'd applied to and been accepted at Macalester College; there he'd be walking into their fine arts building in a month, most likely through snow much deeper and colder than anything he'd known in Kansas. As difficult as he was being about Christmas, she admired him.

Carol drove to the grocery store to buy the ingredients for a Victorian Kansas Fezziwig Feast of cold boiled, cold roast, mince pies, negus, and beer. If they were lucky, Scraps would be home Monday to enjoy some leftovers. In the supermarket Carol found two small roasts and begged the suet for the mince pies. She pushed her cart toward the dried fruit, hoping to find raisins—golden and regular—and currants. Then she'd find the apples, oranges, and lemons, then the almonds, then make her trip to the liquor store for brandy, beer, and the port to make the negus. As always when she grocery shopped, Carol's mind was already home, calculating what needed to be done, anticipating the smells of the beef, the tangy richness of the mince. She stood in front of the raisins. Someone wheeled down the aisle, then stopped behind her.

"The prunes," Laurence said. "Would you mind reaching them for me?"

Carol reached for the prunes. "Pitted?" she asked.

"Most assuredly," said Laurence. "I've had enough pits to last a lifetime."

Carol found a small bag of pitted prunes, or "dried plums" as they'd been rebranded in hopes of attracting a younger demographic.

"And enough petals, too," said Laurence.

Carol turned to him. She put the prunes in his motorized cart.

"I've missed them, actually," said Carol. "Just as I really missed your Cratchit meal."

"But not me?" Laurence smiled up at her, his baggy eyes wrinkling. "Mrs. Cross pulled me through, though we missed you."

"Laurence, you know I've been thinking about you. I'm sorry. But I've had a lot of other things to think about. Finn's been skipping school and walking at all hours. Caldwell . . ." She stopped herself. Why should she bare herself in a grocery-store aisle?

"I read it in the paper. Caldwell's leaving," Laurence said matter-of-factly. "You're taking it hard? Like he's leaving you all over again?"

"I don't know why I should care."

"Yes, why?" said Laurence, sensing her tone. "The big developer, Topeka's salvation, goes to the land of the retired, the elderly, the sun worshipers. The land of little work and easy money. Sounds like him."

"You should let *me* say those things," said Carol.

"He was *my* boss, once. Remember? Can't I dislike him for my own reasons?"

"Of course."

"If you'd let me, I could double-dislike him. My reasons and your reasons." Laurence maneuvered his chair close enough to touch Carol's elbow.

Carol backed away. She wanted to be home. She held tight to her shopping cart.

"You're cooking the Fezziwig meal, are you?" asked Laurence.

Carol nodded and sighed. "You know me well."

"You once invited me to one of your Fezziwig parties. Tried to match me with Freda. Just after my divorce. Years ago, it seems. Back when I could dance. 'Wink with my legs,' to quote your Dickens." Laurence winked with what he was able to, his eye. "So what the dickens is going on this year? Besides feeling scrooged by Caldwell?"

Carol usually appreciated Laurence's wit. "I'm the Scrooge," she admitted. "And you . . . you're Nephew Fred, jolly and persistent, full of invitations." She shoved her cart down the aisle.

Laurence's motorized cart whirred behind her. "Please stop. Just for one second."

Carol let Laurence catch up to her.

"Don't be afraid of what I want," he whispered. "Or of what you need. I've been a mess, I know. I hope to change. I want to find pleasure in life again. I love the pleasure you find in your Christmas meals, in Dickens' Christmas. Is it wrong to want to be part of that? An invitation doesn't have to be an entire future. Damn the future."

"Now you sound like Finn," said Carol.

"I've always liked that boy."

Carol laughed. Laurence was right about her pleasure in Dickens. Could she also find pleasure in Laurence Timmons? How would she ever know the difference between duty and love? "Can you come Sunday night? For the Fezziwig feast?"

"Can Finn pick me up?" asked Laurence.

"No," said Carol. "You'll have to get to my house on your own. Prove that you want to make changes." She started away.

"Time?" Laurence called after her.

"Six," said Carol over her shoulder.

"My pleasure!" shouted Laurence. "Pleasure!" he shouted again.

Carol smiled. Laurence's incessant wit was coming back. Perhaps once his mind found its legs, Laurence would want his body to have legs, too.

Carol loved the Fezziwig feast. Perhaps the Ghost of Christmas Past had said it best: "'twas a small matter to make silly folks so full of gratitude." Yet Scrooge had insisted that the power of a master over apprentices was no small matter at all. Nor was the power Carol might exercise. For six years she'd put fiddle music on the CD player, insisting on dancing with abandon, not even knowing steps, but stepping all the same, whirling like a dervish all through the house. She embarrassed Finn with the manic energy of the evening, but she thought teenage boys *ought* to be embarrassed, again and again, by the women in their lives, until their boyish reticence, their hormonal awkwardness, their damnable self-consciousness, their timidity around bodies and bodily processes were all hammered out of them, and they could ring out their emotions without worrying what anyone else thought. Their embarrassment was like their pimples—a character builder that would disappear as they matured.

But this year had her worried. On Monday Matt Groner would call. How long could Scraps hang on? Would a feast out of Dickens—boiled, roasted, minced—be enough to push Christmas forward? She would have to make it enough. She enjoyed a Saturday afternoon in the kitchen as much as any weekday in her carrel, any Sunday in church. Home from the grocery store, she found a note from Finn. He was at school; jazz band was having a Saturday rehearsal. She unloaded groceries and organized herself.

She started with the rump roast that would become the cold boiled. She immersed the meat in rapidly boiling, salty water to seal in the juices, then put the roast, with some of the water, in the slow cooker. At midnight, she would add onions, carrots, garlic, capers, cloves, peppercorns, bay leaves, basil, oregano, allspice, and nutmeg. The next morning the gray meat would be transferred onto a platter, then put in the refrigerator to cool.

Next Carol trimmed the rib roast, placed it in a very hot oven, reduced the temperature, and cooked it, basting often with its own juices, for the next two hours. She took it out of the oven to let it stand overnight. Like the cold boiled, the cold roast would be put in the refrigerator in the morning. She resisted the temptation to sample: rib roast, cooked in its own juices but still rare, was so tender near the bone. Carol salivated all afternoon. When Finn came home, she fended off his appetite for the meat with an omelet and a salad.

Carol made the mince, and mince she did: raisins, currants, apples, peel, and suet. She added lemon—juice and rind—brandy, sugar, and orange marmalade. Every hour she mixed her mince; each time its pungency increased, until by midnight the mince gripped her nose and would not let go.

Before bed, she started the negus. Carol had debated whether to make Sherry Flip, Sherry Cobbler, Mulled Port, Shrub and Water, Purl, Dog's Nose, or Egg-Hot for Two. But she decided on traditional negus: a bottle of port, a glass of brandy, the juice of one lemon, four ounces of sugar, and three generous pinches of nutmeg. She put everything into a large pitcher. When her Fezziwig feast was served the next day, she would add two pints of boiling water, stir, and drink. Maybe Laurence would appreciate it more than last time. "There's so much that's *not* in it," he had said. "Body, for example. It's thin as Oliver Twist's gruel, as Little Nell's last breath, as Tiny Tim's withered leg. For a punch, it lacks punch." He'd grabbed a Newcastle Ale. Carol had nursed the negus through the next several evenings as her nightcap. This year she'd bought no beer. Laurence would have to abide by her traditions.

At midnight, she called Freda—in Paris it would be seven in the morning—and told her she was keeping Christmas one day at a time, that Scraps was living one day at a time, that one day she might not be so fraught with emotion as she was this year.

"Honey, you're going through a soon-to-be time again," said Freda.

"Soon-to-be what?" asked Carol.

"What do you think? Alone in your house. Back at work after your research grant. With or without Laurence. And then you know what?"

"What?"

"You'll be in some *next* soon-to-be phase."

"I wish you were here to help me get through it," said Carol.

"You don't need me," said Freda.

"The pleasure of your company would be a good thing." The smells of Carol's day in the kitchen swelled, wafted, assaulted her nostrils. "There'll be some good food here."

"As there is here, *mon chéri*," said Freda. "Do not fear. I'll be home soon."

The Fezziwig Meal
Menu

Cold Roast

INGREDIENTS
Roast, rib, 5–8 lbs.

Trim ribs and place joint, standing, in a roasting pan. Preheat oven to 450 degrees and roast for ½ hour, then turn heat down to 350 degrees. Baste frequently. Bake for about ¼ hour per pound. Let sit overnight, then slice into thin pieces.

Cold Boiled

INGREDIENTS
Roast, 1 large brisket or rump
Cloves, 3–6
Peppercorns, 12
Spices, to taste—mustard seed, bay leaf, basil, etc.
Onion, 1, diced
Carrots, 2, cut into rounds
Salt, to taste

Boil beef (with spices, salt, cloves, and peppercorns) for 5 minutes, then simmer 30 minutes per pound. In the last hour, add vegetables. Let stand overnight. Remove beef from broth the next day, slice and serve.

Mincemeat(less) Pies

INGREDIENTS
Raisins, ½ cup
Currants, ½ cup
Suet, 4 oz.
Lemon, ½, rind and juice
Brandy, 3 oz.
Sugar, brown, 5 oz.
Marmalade, orange, 3 tbsp.
Granny Smith apple, 1, cored and chopped
Lime peel, grated

Mince raisins and currants, add lime peel, apple, and orange marmalade. Chop suet finely and add it, along with grated lemon rind, lemon juice, brandy, and sugar. Seal in container and mix each day for a week before making the pies.

Pies: make your favorite pie dough, divide into small balls, roll dough into circles. Dollop on mincemeat and fold over to make half a moon. Slit crust and add more brandy. Cook on slightly oiled baking sheet in 350-degree oven for 30–40 minutes.

Negus (after Cedric Dickens, *Drinking with Dickens*)

INGREDIENTS
Sugar cubes, 8
Lemon, 1
Port, 1 bottle
Brandy, 6–8 oz.
Water, 2 cups, boiled
Nutmeg, grated

Rub sugar cubes against lemon skin until they turn yellow. Put in bowl with juice of lemon and port and add boiling water. Top with nutmeg and serve. Have sugar bowl ready for those who like it sweet.

Beer (if desired)—porter, the same beer the Fezziwig fiddler drowns himself in during a break in the dancing)

"You sure you want lights that high?" Mr. Marble asked Finn. He hoisted his longest ladder off the rack in the carriage house. "Remember, you put them up, you take them down."

"Some people leave them up all year," said Finn.

"Some people are afraid of heights," said Mr. Marble. He poked his head through the ladder rungs, the ladder on his shoulders. "Open the door," he said.

Finn did not move. "My mom's been acting strange."

Mr. Marble waved him away, and Finn swung open the door on its creaky hinges. Old Mr. Marble walked steadily, ten feet of ladder in front of his head, ten feet behind. He grunted past Finn. "Older I get, the more I hate these things."

Finn smiled. Mr. Marble had refused to hang lights the day before. He wanted a day of sunshine to melt the snow. "I'll go up," said Finn.

"Ever been up that high?" Mr. Marble flipped the ladder over his head and set it on the ground. "Help me walk it up," he said.

Finn joined him midway in the ladder's length, and they

hoisted it to vertical. Mr. Marble pulled the nylon rope and extended the ladder so high that Finn almost stumbled backward looking up. "I can do it," Finn said.

"Young people," said Mr. Marble. "Weren't for foolishness wouldn't anything happen in this world." Finn knew Marble was ready to talk. "Meanwhile, your mother gets strange. And I hate ladders. So it's your turn to do the work." Mr. Marble walked the ladder slowly toward the chimney. He let the top of it drop onto the bricks, then checked the rubber feet. They were even. "Up to you," he said.

Finn climbed, lights over his shoulder, duct tape hanging on one wrist. The star for the chimney top was attached to his belt loop. He climbed until if he went any farther, he'd lose the upper ladder rails to hang onto. He looked down at the top of Mr. Marble's hat, at the little red feather stuck in the brim. The old man raised his head. "Higher when you're up high, isn't it?" the old man sang out.

Finn looked up instead of down. Marble had given him a large clamp for the star. "Just clip it to the little metal chimney roof I put up there after your skunks moved away," he'd instructed Finn.

Finn reached over the top of the chimney to clip the star, which was made of many little pointed bulbs. People would see it from the street, shining all night through the season. He looked over the top of his house at the other neighborhood roofs. His would be the highest light, because they had the tallest chimney. The street had a couple of brick Victorians in the middle, some airplane bungalows on either side, some prairie foursquares toward the end of the block, and, across the street, some one-story cottages. Some yards were bare, some toy-strewn, some planted in bushes, some in grass; some were fenced, to keep in children and dogs, and some doubled as driveways and parking spaces. In the crisp air, Finn saw every detail, and even though many of the details were ugly, they were fine with him. When Caldwell lived with them, he complained about the neighborhood. Carol always said, "I love the house, so I'm going to love the neighborhood that makes the house affordable."

"A junkyard is a junkyard, even if you find a jewel in it," his father always replied.

Finn thought everyone should do just as they wanted. Some people mowed their grass, others let it grow. Some painted their houses, some let them peel. Some maintained their brick sidewalks, others let weeds split wide cracks. Some gardened flowers, some vegetables, while others used their backyards to collect derelict cars.

Finn looked at his own roof, his own yard, at the carriage house. He had to admit that what Carol called a "jewel" had lost some of its sparkle. The back fence was ready to fall in. The carriage house listed like a drunk. The yard was strewn with the leaves he was supposed to rake, revealed once more after the snow melted. And the shingles on the roof were mealy, crumbling, almost bare of the small chit their maker had pressed into the asphalt. At least he was doing something to make the house look better for the season. Finn grabbed the cord from the bottom of the star and climbed down several rungs.

"The star!" Mr. Marble yelled up at him.

"What?" Finn asked.

"The star. You want one of the points up, don't you?"

Finn climbed up a couple of rungs. The five-pointed star was shaped like the ones he'd had in his room all those years before. And, yes, Finn had clipped the star with two points up, and even. "A star doesn't know what's up or down, does it?" he shouted to Mr. Marble. He climbed to where he could plug the star into the string of lights and wrap them around the chimney until he came to the roof line. Then he notched the cords along the sides, as Mr. Marble had suggested, with a twist and a small piece of duct tape to hold them against the mortar. "Come down easier that way, too," Mr. Marble had said. Finn worked his way down, making wide and narrow Xs, sometimes making Zs. He'd bought four strings, with big bulbs. The chimney would be a riot of color. At the bottom of the ladder Mr. Marble waited with the extension cord.

Finn plugged in the combined string of lights. They glowed weakly in the midafternoon sun. He couldn't tell if the star was shining at all.

"You said something about your mother?" asked Mr. Marble.

"She's watching me all the time. She's upset about my dad moving, and me leaving next month. She has to have everything just so, like if you don't do every single thing just like you did it before, you'll get some kind of Christmas curse."

"The Christmas curse," said Mr. Marble. "I've seen many come under its spell."

"Like a horror movie, huh?" said Finn.

"Worse. Like real life," said Mr. Marble.

Finn nodded. He walked toward the house but stopped when he heard the clatter of the extension ladder, the top coming down rung by cacophonous rung. He helped Mr. Marble walk the ladder back down, then he hurried over to the carriage house door. "Talk to her, for God's sake," Mr. Marble muttered as he puffed by with the ladder riding his shoulders. The old man flipped it onto its hook on the wall, then shook his head. "Nobody talks anymore," he said. "Everybody's busy with their secrets."

Finn started to leave the carriage house.

"So?" asked Mr. Marble. "When are you going to talk to her? About your secrets?"

"I don't know. Most adults . . . I mean, I trust you . . . but they step in and take over. They don't let you do anything by yourself."

Mr. Marble nodded. "Your mother's not *most* adults any more than I am," he said.

Finn shrugged. "Thanks for the advice," he said, running into the house.

Carol wondered if she should invite Mr. Marble to stay for dinner. Laurence would like the old chimney sweep. She'd called Laurence twice already. The first time to double-check that he was really coming, the second to offer Finn's services as chauffeur after all.

"You're not as concerned about my independence as you were in the store?" Laurence teased her.

"I want you here," Carol said.

"I'll find my way," said Laurence. "Finn has enough to do helping you get ready."

"He's outside putting a star on the chimney," said Carol.

"I'll follow that star of wonder, star of might, star with royal beauty bright."

"You'll be coming east, not west," said Carol.

"And I'll be the wiser for it," said Laurence.

"Stop," said Carol.

"You used to like my puns," he said. "You used to like me."

"I invited you to dinner, didn't I?" asked Carol.

"Don't act incensed," Laurence said. "Frankly, I'll be there, bearing gold and mirth."

Carol huffed her disapproval of more puns and hung up. Cleverness was good, but sometimes overwhelmed what she hoped was Laurence's serious intent to change, to quit being so dependent, to quit moping and get on with his life. Outside, the ladder came down. She looked out the window, glad to see Finn safe on the ground.

She went to the kitchen to finish her Fezziwig feast. She doubled her butter-crust recipe for the mince pies. She cut flour into butter, added salt and a small bit of sugar and a touch of cream of tartar, then worked the dough smooth with her hands. She rolled out small balls to create flat circles a little bigger than her hand. She spooned generous portions of mince on each, then brought the dough together and pinched the edges into little half-moons. Some years Finn and she had dared each other to eat one more small pie, and then another and another until neither could move from the table. She slit each pie and poured brandy in the slits of the pies she and Laurence would eat. She carried her baking sheet to the waiting oven, then sat for a moment of rest.

Finn banged into the kitchen. He peered into the oven. "Just starting to brown," he said. "You'll need someone to test quality, won't you?"

"They'll be fine," said Carol.

"Laurence still coming?" he asked. "He can be a little picky, right?"

"You're not getting pie until dinner," Carol said.

"What's for lunch?" asked Finn.

"Can of soup for me. You want me to fix you a sandwich?" Carol went to the refrigerator. A scraping sound outside drove her to the kitchen window. Mr. Marble had found a rake in the carriage house and was going after the leaves. "Finn, go tell Mr. Marble to leave those leaves alone. That's your job. By now, you should be ashamed of them."

"He likes to work," said Finn.

"Get out there this minute. Just take the rake and do the work. I'll fix you lunch while you do it."

"I'm starving," Finn said.

"It's an hour's worth of work. Half an hour if you hurry."

"I'll tell him to leave," said Finn. He went to the refrigerator and opened the door. "I could try the cold boiled, with mayonnaise and pickles." Finn reached for the ingredients. "There's tons," he added.

"Out," said Carol.

Soon, Finn's voice drifted in from the yard, and the sound of raking stopped. Finn came back into the house. "He's gone," Finn said.

"You're not raking?" asked Carol.

"Mom, I'm starving. I promise I'll do it soon. Really."

"Go wash your hands," Carol said.

The phone rang. Finn found the portable phone on the dining table. Carol couldn't tell who Finn was talking to, because he wasn't saying much, just, "yeah" and "sure" and "okay." Somehow, Carol expected the worst. She finished preparing his sandwich, then sliced one more thin piece of cold boiled for herself. God, it was tasty.

She carried Finn's plate into the dining room and went back to the kitchen to pour him some milk. When Finn put the phone down, he half smiled at Carol. "Dad wants to take me shopping this afternoon. I said okay. You look like you're on top of everything here." Finn took a bite of the sandwich. "Way on top," he said, his mouth full. "This is great."

Carol went back into the kitchen and made coffee. She opened a can of chicken soup and put it in a saucepan. The oven timer dinged. She peered through the glass. The mince pies looked perfect. She put on an oven mitt and pulled out the first tray. She loaded in the sheet with the remaining pies. She removed the flaky, lightly browned half circles to a waiting plate. The steam from the slits rose to her nose. She picked up a pie and carried it into the dining room to Finn's plate. Finn smiled. "I'll get to the leaves real soon," he said.

"Enjoy your father," Carol said. "But don't you dare be late for dinner. Tell him Laurence is coming. If he asks, you can tell him I don't want the land, or the loft."

"You're not going to move when I go away to college?" Finn asked.

"I'll be right here," Carol said. "You know that."

Finn finished his lunch and went upstairs to change his clothes. Mr. Marble had told him to talk to his mother, but he couldn't. Carol wouldn't understand. Her Christmas didn't leave room for anything but her own preoccupations.

He yelled good-bye as he hurried down the stairs. He slammed the door behind him. The day had warmed to a promised forty-five degrees. Finn unzipped his sweatshirt jacket. He looked once again at the lights he'd strung. In just a few hours they'd be lit against the night, all those zigzags leading to a star. Finn started down the street, turned east on Third, and picked up his pace. He had to be at the church by one thirty. They'd warm up for half an hour, then play at two. Teresa had promised to have him on his way by four. He'd left his trumpet with her so Carol wouldn't ask any questions. He felt a twinge of guilt for lying, but he had his own Christmas plans.

Folklórica had asked him to play for a *quinceañera*, something Finn had never heard of before. The event would be in the basement of Our Lady of Guadalupe Church. One of the trumpet players had to be family instead of musician—his sister was the one celebrating her fifteenth birthday. The *quinceañera* was her coming out. "Like a bat mitzvah for a Jewish girl or a debutante ball for a Texas girl," Teresa had explained. Finn walked quickly toward the church, excited and nervous about his first time playing mariachi in public. He had picked up the music quickly enough, those few harmony parts they'd relegated to him, but he knew from experience that rehearsal was different from performance. And, it wasn't just how *he* would do. Everyone was different in public. He'd had band directors who stayed calm through months of rehearsal, then rushed mercilessly through a piece on performance night. He'd seen kids faint, violin strings break, trumpet valves jam, clarinet keys fall off, drum skins explode. On the way to the church he told himself what his best bandleader, Mrs. Hein from middle school, always said, "Just do your part, because you sure can't do anyone else's."

Teresa greeted him at the basement door of the church with a cobbled costume. "From all the ones who have played with us for a little while, then left for school," she said. The closest fit in pants seemed too tight. "You're used to those baggy pants. All the boys are," said Teresa. "The traditional clothes, they show the body." The jacket was too large in the chest, too long in the sleeves. "You will pass," said Teresa. "Especially with this." She handed Finn a large sombrero studded with silver that weighed heavily on his head.

Finn warmed up his trumpet, then they tuned. They played the first half of one of their standard numbers. "We'll stick to slow ones for today," Teresa said to Finn. "We have one set, then we are welcome to the refreshments. Then another set at the end. We are the beginning and the end."

Finn thought of parentheses, of his mother, counting punctuation. She'd never mentioned parentheses. He'd ask her why not. If she counted them, why didn't she speak of it? He wasn't really sure he wanted to get her started. Finn liked parentheses. In his music he often saw phrases (literally inside phrases) that were both amplification and aside.

They marched into the big hall underneath the sanctuary and lined up to play. Finn found his place. He thought Gabriela would be in the audience, but he couldn't find her. Once Folklórica started into their first number, Finn felt at home. They played with such confidence. His parts were small and routine—the staccato embellishment, the occasional emphasis of the melody, the fanfare beginnings and endings. Finn joined the rest of Folklórica in their easy style, their sureness, their infectious enjoyment of the music they could make. As Teresa had promised, they played slow numbers, and though Finn made at least twenty mistakes, he remembered what Mr. Riley always told him: "In any other pursuit, hitting ninety-nine percent would be astounding."

After the set Folklórica went backstage. Teresa exhorted them to be ready to play after eating some cake and visiting with friends. Finn hesitated to go back into the hall. "They will welcome you," Teresa promised. She left Finn alone.

Just as Finn started toward the door, someone hurried into the room, almost knocking him down.

"I have been wanting to talk to you," said a short man with a large belly.

Gabriela's father, Finn guessed, but he'd only seen the man once, at night, on his roof and climbing down a ladder. Finn stood silent.

"My daughter," the man said, "interested in the music again. And the boys."

"I saw Gabriela at Rosaria's one day. Her aunt Teresa was there, too. Gabriela told her I play the trumpet." Finn moved toward his horn, as though it might protect him. He picked it up. "I'm interested in the music. That's all."

The man advanced, then paced in front of Finn. "So, I am to believe . . ." he began, and he turned and took Finn's trumpet with a quick swipe of his hand, "you play the music, but you don't play with my Gabriela . . ." He held the trumpet exactly as someone would who knew the instrument well. He pumped the keys up and down the scale. "And all this meeting is by accident?"

Finn reached for his trumpet.

"You do not think I know who you are?" asked Gabriela's father. "Who your father is?" He held the trumpet as high in the air as he could. When Finn extended his arms for it, the short man punched him in the stomach.

Finn doubled and fell. He took shallow breaths. Gabriela's father kneeled and put the trumpet next to Finn's ear. "Next time," he whispered, "I go for the cojones." He raised his voice. "The same cojones that made a whore of my daughter."

The door opened. Finn raised his head and breathed deeply. He was not badly hurt. The old blind man Juan, Rosaria's father, tapped his way into the room. He stopped when he reached Gabriela's father. "Cojones, Roberto?" asked Juan. He lifted his cane to point it at Roberto. "You have cojones? And you use them to hit your son?"

"He is not *my* son," Roberto spat.

"If he is not your son, then you must admit that he is not responsible for Gabriela."

Roberto stood up. "*Viejo*," he said and walked out of the room.

Finn unfolded himself. He sat up, holding his stomach. "I didn't do anything," Finn said, sounding to himself like a whiny ten-year-old.

"You are a friend," said Juan. "Roberto does not understand. He has no friends. You must continue to teach him."

"He'll hit me again," said Finn. He grabbed his trumpet and stood up.

"He will not, *hijo*," said Juan. "I will see to that." The old man tapped toward the door.

Finn put his trumpet in its case, then went into the bathroom where he'd left his regular clothes. He couldn't go back out and play if Roberto was there. He changed and left through a back exit, climbing the stairwell with some dread. Roberto could be waiting for him outside. Finn thought of himself lying on the basement floor, doubled up, the shape of a parenthesis. He *was* a small aside, of no real importance. Roberto was so angry. Should he quit seeing Gabriela? But Juan had called him "hijo" and "friend." The pain in his stomach eased as he walked home.

Carol liked to know when Finn was seeing his father. At first, there'd been the terms of the divorce. Caldwell "got" Finn every other weekend and for a week in the summer. After the first couple of years, when Caldwell became busy with his development projects and was traveling out of state, and the emotional rancor over the divorce had dissipated, Carol and Caldwell amicably worked out a schedule month by month. Then, at sixteen, Finn learned to drive, and Carol couldn't always know where Finn might be. Once he came home with beer on his breath. "Dad says one beer isn't going to kill me," Finn said. Once he came home with a new T-shirt, some hideous thing that could only be appreciated in the black light of Finn's room. "Turns out Dad likes Metallica," Finn said. Another time he came home with a tiger fish and an inadequate bowl. "Isn't it cool?" Finn asked. The fish died within the week.

So when Finn came home exhausted in the late afternoon on the day of their Fezziwig feast, trumpet case in hand, Carol questioned him. "Didn't your father drive you home?"

"I wanted to walk," said Finn.

"Why do you have your trumpet?" Carol asked.

"I wanted to play him something," said Finn. He set his trumpet case next to the piano, then brightened up. "Dad wants me to fly to Arizona with him. Sometime after Christmas, for a week."

"Absolutely not," said Carol.

"We'll be back in time for me to leave for school. We worked it all out." Finn pushed past her. He took off his jacket and hung it on the hook in the hall.

"No," Carol said.

"I really want to go," said Finn.

"What about Scraps?" asked Carol.

Finn hung his head. "You'll do anything to get me to stay," he said.

"I can't believe you're saying that," said Carol.

Finn ran up the stairs. His door slammed shut. The phone rang. Carol's terse "Hello" turned out to be appropriate.

"You sound happy," Caldwell said.

Carol chose silence.

"Is something wrong?" asked Caldwell.

"He's not going," said Carol.

"What?" asked Caldwell.

"You know damn well what. Arizona. He's not going."

"You sure have a definite opinion about nothing," said Caldwell. "Did you want to know why *I* called?"

Carol hung up. A trip to Arizona was not nothing. She took a deep breath and thought of her best strategy. She marched up to Finn's room and told him she wouldn't stand in his way. "Even though I thought we were having a full Christmas together," she reminded him.

"*You* are," said Finn. "It's your Christmas." He lay on the bed, facing the wall.

"You don't have to be smart aleck," said Carol.

"It'd just be for a week," said Finn. He turned over to face her. He reached for the side of the bed and pulled himself up to sit on the edge. "We'd still have Christmas together. Just not New Year's." He bent forward.

"Is something wrong with you?" asked Carol. "Did you hurt yourself?"

"I'm fine," said Finn.

"You don't act fine," said Carol. "You look pale."

"I tripped. I tried to protect my trumpet. I fell on the case. Right in the stomach." Finn bent forward, then lay back down.

Carol approached the bed. "Let me see," she said.

"Just leave me alone."

"Like you want to leave *me* alone?" asked Carol. "Usually we go through Epiphany."

"I'd be back right after New Year's. Way before Epiphany. To take down the decorations and the tree and everything else."

"You decide," said Carol. She was more upset at Caldwell than Finn. "You'll be here tonight?"

"For your Fezziwig meal," Finn said.

"*Our* Fezziwig feast. You didn't even want another pie when you came in."

"I'm not hungry," said Finn.

"Do you miss Scraps?" she asked. "You always fed him. Even before yourself."

"Of course I miss Scraps, Mom," said Finn. "Just because I might go to Arizona doesn't mean I don't care about Scraps. Or about you." He stood up and sniffed the air. "I love the smell of those pies," he said. He moved to Carol's side and let her give him a hug. "I'll be hungry soon."

"Good," said Carol. "Laurence will be here any minute."

Finally, a taxi pulled into their drive and Laurence wheeled himself into the house. Carol brought out the negus and Laurence drank with gusto. When Carol reminded him he hadn't liked it before, Laurence asked, "Can't we change?"

Carol sighed, then remembered her Dickens: Having some power toward making the evening "happy or unhappy, light or burdensome, pleasure or toil," all from the smallest "words and looks—things so slight and insignificant that it is impossible to add and count 'em up."

They brought out the cold boiled, and Carol cut the meat as thin as she could, until Laurence thought he could cut it thinner, which he did, until Finn insisted he could cut it thinnest of all, and Carol salted hers, and Laurence peppered his, and Finn ate his plain, and Carol brought out the cold roast, which they kept on the bone, enjoying the chance to use their fingers, enjoying the tearing of flesh still pink at the bone, wiping their hands on Carol's large Christmas napkins before taking another swig of negus, though Finn kept his to half a cup, the negus complementing the mince pies as though they'd been born twins, and at some point negus had decided to become liquid and mince solid, and the flaky crust of the pies crumbed Laurence's well-trimmed beard and dropped to their plates and to the floor, and Carol rose to put on the fiddle music she'd readied for the occasion, and she couldn't help but spin and skip, hop and turn, her calves, as Dickens wrote, shining "like moons," and Finn couldn't help but rise from his chair and cut a few steps himself, and Laurence backed his wheelchair away and clapped his hands and shook his head and, surprising Carol, gave a cheery whoop of pleasure at seeing mother and son dance, which they did through two jigs, until their giddiness, as diminished as their breath, dissipated, and they sat again and found new appetite for the simple food.

Later, as his cab pulled into Carol's driveway, Laurence said, "Nothing finer than abandoning yourself to the right things. And all of the evening was right. The company. The food. The music. The dance. Thank you."

Carol bent to his chair. She kissed his cheek.

"So chaste?"

"The end of the evening," said Carol. "Perhaps we will have others."

"Indeed," said Laurence. The cab driver approached the porch, and Laurence signaled Carol away. She knew he did not want her to see the laborious process she had helped him through so many times: the leaning back of the chair, the gentle (and sometimes not so gentle) stair-by-stair lowering of chair to sidewalk, then to the cab, then the swing inside.

Finn was on the phone, nearly shouting. "I'm coming. Book it." And, after a pause, "Mom let me decide." Finn came into the dining room, where Carol was clearing the table. "Dad says to tell you 'good call.'"

"*I* made the right decision," said Carol.

Finn brought food and empty plates to the kitchen. Carol ran water in the sink.

When the phone rang, she let Finn answer. He listened, then hung up. "Red-eye flight. The middle of the night," Finn reported. "He says we'll be fine because we're night owls."

"What about your sleep?" Carol asked.

"You mean *your* sleep," said Finn.

Finn dropped the last of the silverware in the dishwater and went to his room. Carol couldn't believe he was really going, but then Caldwell could be as persuasive as he was permissive. Most likely, this would be the first of many trips to Arizona, if Finn and Caldwell were to see each other. But leave it to Caldwell to pick such a time to ask, and to win Finn's consent. She stored the food, finished the dishes, and started up the stairs.

When his mother tapped on his door, Finn didn't answer. When she opened the door, and a crack of light from the hall climbed quickly up his wall, Finn pulled his blanket up to his chin. He didn't want Carol to see his black jeans, his charcoal sweatshirt jacket.

"You've been leaving the house," she said. "Even though I asked you not to."

"Not every night," said Finn.

She came into his room. "What do you do out there?"

"I just like to walk, okay? And think. I don't do anything wrong."

"You're not happy?" Carol asked.

"I was happy tonight," said Finn. "Weren't you?"

Carol put her hand to her mouth, as though to signal silence. That was their rule, wasn't it? Especially during Christmas, the season of good cheer? Finn was sorry he'd asked her about her happiness, because he knew that if she were honest, she wouldn't leave his room for an hour. He'd miss his walk, miss seeing Gabriela, and maybe, in spite of all his plans, this would be the very night she'd need him.

"I liked seeing Laurence," Finn said.

"He liked seeing you. He's been trying hard this Christmas, too," said Carol.

"I don't need another father," Finn said.

"You need a friend. We all do." Carol sat on the edge of his bed.

"You're right, Mom," he said. He turned to the wall. All around the crack of light from the hall Finn's fluorescent galaxy glowed. Some nights Finn watched those stars all the way to when they lost their stored energy and faded into blackness.

"Maybe I should have asked which of your friends *you'd* like to invite over," said Carol.

"Don't worry," said Finn. "I like Laurence. I'll invite someone to the big Christmas meal. Maybe Mr. Marble, since he helped me put up the lights."

"Not someone your own age? Maybe the girl you've been helping?" Carol put a hand on his shoulder.

Finn turned to look at her. "Don't worry."

She nodded.

"It's okay if you like Laurence," said Finn. "He's kind of cool."

Carol rose from the bed. "Stay home tonight," she said.

"I am," said Finn. Carol left the room. He'd have to skip part of school the next day. Mondays were low-key anyway. Gabriela could have her baby any day.

As soon as Carol was in her room, Finn took off his clothes, put on his pajamas, and crawled back into bed. Gabriela would be in her bed, too, in the small room at the back of her little house. Outside her windows the Christmas lights her father had strung across the roof and along the guttering would glow like a nightlight, enough for her to see the cross on her wall: Jesus crucified, nailed, tortured, triumphant. He would redeem everyone through his suffering, though he could not *stop* anyone's suffering. Gabriela lay swollen with child, huge, and tortured by the guilt her father flogged her with, and her father, in the next room, lay tortured by what he considered his family shame, that a daughter would be pregnant with no boy to marry, and her *abuela* lay in the converted closet, just big enough for a cot, windowless and darker than a thousand moonless Mexican nights, wondering what might become of her *hijo*, her *nieta*, their casa, with its for sale sign stuck in the yard, announcing to everyone that soon they would have to move, as they had so many times before. How many more times would they have to move? When would they find a real home? Finn lay in his bed, his stomach just beginning to bruise around the redness that marked Roberto's punch.

In one month Finn would find his new home, a dormitory room. His father would move. His mother? She would move, too, though she could be a glacier.

monday, december 22

Finn and Gabriela waited while Rosaria shooed away some *viejos* who spent their mornings drinking coffee. She pointed to Gabriela's condition, shaming them to give up their seats. A busboy cleared the table. On their way to the register, the old ones stopped before Rosaria's father, Juan, the blind one. One man dropped coins in a cup. When he heard the sound, *el ciego* raised his head and asked, "*¿Quién es?*" Then he leaned forward and whispered something in the man's bent ear. The other old men repeated the offering and heard whatever *el ciego* said.

During Christmas week, Gabriela explained, the old man was called upon for his second sight. He was said to share the future with each receptive ear. "I'll try him," said Finn. He took two quarters from his pocket and went to the old man's table, dropping them noisily into the cup.

"*¿Quién es?*"

"Finn Dickens-Dunmore. Gabriela's friend. Thank you for helping me yesterday at the church."

The old man curled his finger and Finn leaned forward. The

old man spoke rapidly in Spanish. "*La paz del mundo*," he said, "*es en las sonrisas, las piernas y las palabras de los niños. Tu hijo es mi hijo y nuestros hijos son los hijos del mundo.*"

"*Gracias*," said Finn. He had no idea what the old man had told him.

"Please," said the old man, finding Finn's hand and holding it. "Tell Gabriela that her house is sold. A new owner will visit with her father on the day after Christmas."

"Is that bad?" Finn tried to remove his hand, but the old man held it close.

"She will not lose a home."

"Why do you speak Spanish to me, but give me the message for Gabriela in English?" asked Finn. He sat down next to Juan.

The old man smiled. "When you must know what to tell her, I speak that in English. And when you must *learn* what I am telling you, I speak that in Spanish. *¿Comprende?*"

"*Sí*," said Finn.

"I have told you a lullaby. *Una canción de cuna*," said *el ciego*. "Teresa will sing it to you." He let go of Finn's hand. "*Vaya con* Gabriela."

"*Gracias*," said Finn again.

Gabriela had almost finished the basket of chips. Finn dipped several in Rosaria's salsa—chunky with tomatoes, full of cilantro, rich with onion and garlic, hot with small bits of serrano pepper. "Your house has been sold," he said after he'd drunk some water.

"Juan told you that?" asked Gabriela. She pushed the basket of chips toward Finn and put her hands under the table.

Their server came toward them. "Usual?" she asked.

Gabriela and Finn nodded. Finn would eat all his tamales today since Scraps was still at Dr. Groner's. He wondered when they'd hear.

"Juan says you won't have to move." Finn ate more chips.

"How does he know?" asked Gabriela.

"Second sight, you said," Finn reminded her.

"What else did he say?" Gabriela reached for a chip.

"Something about a lullaby," Finn said to Gabriela. "He said Teresa would know it. I'll ask her at the next mariachi practice."

"The one with the *sonrisas, piernas y palabras*?" asked Gabriela.

"I think so," said Finn.

"She's been teaching me," said Gabriela. "She wrote it herself, I think."

"Will you sing it to me?" asked Finn.

"Not here," said Gabriela.

"Please?"

"*Cante, hija*," said *el ciego* from across the room. Rosaria came with their food. "*Cante*," she said. Rosaria started the song, softly, and Gabriela joined in, her voice a whisper. From across the room, the old man spoke along.

¿Dónde está la paz de nuestro mundo
Y dónde . . . encontrarla?
Unas veces en la sonrisa de mi hijo;
Espero sonrisas fuertes para el mundo.

¿Dónde está la paz de nuestro mundo
Y dónde . . . encontrarla?
Unas veces en las piernas de mi hijo;
Espero piernas fuertes para el mundo.

¿Dónde está la paz de nuestro mundo
Y dónde . . . encontrarla?

Unas veces en las palabras de mi hijo;
Espero palabras fuertes para el mundo.

Porque si sus sonrisas, piernas y palabras
Son fuertes tendrán poder para traer paz;
Cuando los niños son hermanos y hermanas
El mundo va a aprender a dar gracias.

Sonrisas fuertes vienen de corazones de oro,
Y piernas fuertes de un cuerpo sano,
Y palabras fuertes de un cerebro listo;
Espero esto para los niños del mundo.

¿Dónde está la paz de nuestro mundo
Y dónde . . . encontrarla?
Cuando tratamos a cada niño como a mi hijo,
Los hijos serán los mejores padres del mundo.

Rosaria left the table. Gabriela, at first flushed with embarrassment at the song, was suddenly pale. She stared at her plate. "I was always so hungry. The last few days, not so much."

"Eat what you can. That's what my mother always tells me," said Finn.

"You'll take home what I can't eat?" asked Gabriela.

"I wish Scraps was there. I wish he was hungry." Finn tore the husks off his chicken tamal and ate half of it in two large bites. "What does the song mean?" Finn asked.

Rosaria came back to check on them. "You're not eating," she said to Gabriela.

"And she's not telling me about the song. What it means," said Finn.

Rosaria crossed her arms. "It means the only true peace in

the world comes when a child is treated well. When a child is allowed to grow. First comes the smiles, then the crawling and the walking, and then the words start to come. It's a wish for health. For all the children of the world."

"Will Teresa give me the words?" Finn asked Rosaria and Gabriela.

"I have the words." Gabriela stood up. "I'll find them when you walk me home."

"Do you want a box?" asked Rosaria.

"Two boxes," said Finn. He finished the rest of his unwrapped tamal. Gabriela remained standing. "Are you all right?" he asked her.

"I'm pregnant," she whispered to him.

He almost laughed, but when he saw tears welling in her eyes he reached for her hand. "You're going to be fine."

"I'm not myself anymore." Gabriela let go of Finn's hand and sat down. She picked at her food. "I just wish it was all over."

"Soon it will be," said Finn. "I'll help you."

"Promise?" asked Gabriela.

"I've got a plan," Finn said. "If you can just hold on until the day after Christmas, I'll have a place for you. A whole week with nobody to wonder where I am. Or to try to find you."

"Promise?" asked Gabriela.

Rosaria came back to the table and boxed their food. When they went to the cash register, Rosaria waved them away. "*Vayan con Dios*," she said.

"*Gracias*," said Gabriela and Finn together.

Finn put a dollar in the old man's cup. *El ciego* leaned forward, and Finn edged closer to him. "Promise," whispered the old man. "Promise her."

"I promise," said Finn.

Finn walked Gabriela home. He helped her over the missing

step onto her porch. "Here." He handed her the boxes of food. "In case you get hungry." Finn wondered if someone was inside, her *abuela*, watching, either approving or disapproving. Gabriela went inside, but before Finn turned to walk away, she opened the door to hand him a sheet of scribbled words. The lullaby. "Thanks," he said and stuffed it in his pocket.

"*Adiós*," said Gabriela and shut the door.

Finn jumped off the porch and walked to the street. He stared at the tiny house. Something was different. Finn smiled. The for sale sign was gone. Without it, the yard looked bare. Something else was different. Finn looked at the roof. No porch stair lay where Roberto had tossed it. Maybe the new owner would fix the stairs.

Finn walked over the Branner Street Bridge to Sixth Street, then toward downtown Topeka. Soon the cathedral tower of Topeka High School showed itself through the holes in Topeka's inconsistent skyline. Opened in 1931—Topekans love to claim, with indifference to fact, that it was the first million-dollar high school built west of the Mississippi—the school, with its vaulted, Tudor-beamed library, its greenhouses, its auditorium with ornate chandeliers and massive velvet curtains, its halls of marble and walnut, was constructed as a Gothic cathedral to education. Finn shoved his hands into his jacket pockets and lowered his head. He might just make it to this cathedral of a school before his free period and his independent study were over. He wished his mother would let him use the car, but, as she always said, "You're mobile enough already."

In the Ramada Inn parking lot, Finn saw Mr. Marble's truck. Maybe the sweep was inside, having lunch at the restaurant. Maybe he was working there. His ladders were secure, though, and his brushes. Finn walked to the truck, in case Mr. Marble was inside and he could hitch a ride to Topeka High. Finn came close enough to peek in. Mr. Marble lay on the seat, his feet under the steering wheel, his hat a crumpled cushion for his head where it lay propped against the passenger door. Mr. Marble looked terribly uncomfortable, and for a moment Finn wondered if he was still breathing. He almost rapped on the window, but Mr. Marble's hand twitched against the seat, and his chest heaved. Finn decided to move on. Finn noticed an old board, rotten, once painted green, in the back of the truck. Gabriela's step.

Carol played hooky from her study carrel. To assuage her guilt she outlined her research plan for the week Finn would be in Arizona. She would move her study of punctuation past the transition from the Victorian (Charles Dickens) to the Modern (D. H. Lawrence) and look at writers like James Joyce and William Faulkner, who had practiced the seemingly new innovations of stretched sentences and stream of consciousness, their focus on the concentrated interiors of their characters as a substitute for the broad exteriors, the web of society, the definite actions of characters in the Victorian novels of Dickens and Thackeray. These innovators sometimes gave up that most basic punctuation, the space, content to write words and then decide whether to punctuate them or *justjamthemtogether* as though *languagewereonlythought* and not *writtencommunication*. They were undoubtedly great writers, though they seemed to care so little for their readers. At the same time Hemingway had stripped sentences to such simplicity that Faulkner said his fellow writer feared sending a reader to a dictionary. Carol found equal richness under the surface of a Hemingway story as in the stream of consciousness of Faulkner's Benjy and Joyce's Molly Bloom. But all three writers forced the reader to either dig or sort. In such literature anything and everything is possible—everything, that is, except for the direct contact with the reader that the Victorians practiced.

Carol wasn't sure when she'd finish her counting. The process *was* tedious, but counting was only part of what she did; she also read to see the why and wherefore of the punctuation. So, she would continue reading and counting until she'd thought of all the questions she might ask, and how she might answer them.

Except for the expected phone call about Scraps, Carol looked forward to the next few days, dominated by Finn's schedule: a band concert that evening; a jazz band swing night on Tuesday. Then Finn would be home for Christmas Eve Day. By then, surely, he'd find the Christmas spirit? After outlining her research, Carol took care of business past: she wrote to her ex-husband.

Caldwell:

You were never charmed by this house, but it's mine, and I'll remain here until I can no longer negotiate the stairs. This place has been as steady and warm and adaptable as I wish all my other relationships could have been. If it's in need of work, well, that too is no different from any relationship. I'll find the time and the money. Frankly, I don't care what you do with your loft. You are free to sell it to someone who might be attracted by your lofty ideas for Downtown Topeka development.

As you divest yourself and make the move to Arizona—I do hope you have a good time there with Finn—you don't have to take me into consideration any more than you ever have. Finn probably told you I don't want the Auburn Road property; you always said we bought it for Finn as much as for ourselves, and, as its value is not so great that you'd need to sell it right away, you might wait to talk to Finn about its disposal. In the meantime, I wish you whatever joys of the holiday you will find.

Carol

By the time she took the letter to the mailbox, she found her day's mail. Nothing from Laurence. He hadn't called, either. He'd simply taken his leave after the Fezziwig meal and disappeared. Laurence had trouble being straightforward—buying all those flowers instead of declaring his thanks, his desire for change, his possible love; then he sent the petals instead of talking directly about the future. But as she returned from the mailbox with nothing but junk mail, solicitations to charity, and a credit card bill—plus the letter to Caldwell she'd not put out in time—Carol rebuked herself. She hadn't been completely honest and straightforward with Laurence. She was not only disappointed but angry that he didn't want to go back to work, that he refused to give the prostheses a chance, that he would not outfit his car for handicapped driving. As he ignored those things, he ignored her. Yet she was ignoring him, as well.

Carol went to the phone, determined to have her say with Laurence. Before she could touch the key pad, the phone rang in her hand. She hoped it might be Laurence, preempting her need to call him. Then she felt the dread of a call from Matt Groner. "Hello?" she asked.

A hesitant voice, a woman, slightly accented, said, "Is this the mother of the boy Finn?"

"This is Carol Dickens," said Carol. "Finn Dickens-Dunmore is my son. Is everything all right?"

"That is why I am calling *you*," said the voice. "I am Teresa. He has spoken of me?"

Carol tried to recall the name. "I'm afraid I don't remember," she said.

"But he is okay?" asked Teresa. "When he left early, saying nothing, I became frightened. Juan said he had been hit in the stomach, but he was okay today."

Carol took a deep breath. "What are you talking about? When *was* this?"

"Yesterday. The *quinceañera*. The mariachi band played. My band, Folklórica."

"Finn was with his father Sunday afternoon," said Carol. "They planned a trip."

"He went to his father, then? After he was hit? After he played with us?"

Finn had said something about a fall. He'd been carrying his trumpet case. "I'm sorry," Carol said. "He did tell me he was practicing with your mariachi band. He didn't say he'd been with you yesterday. But he's fine. He came home. We talked. We had a family dinner together. He even danced."

"Thanks be to God," said Teresa. "I am sorry to bother you."

"No bother." Carol hesitated. "I'm glad you called. Can you call me before you perform next? I'd love to hear you."

"I am sorry to tell you things Finn has not told you himself. I don't want to make trouble for him. He is a nice boy. He has been good to our Gabriela."

Carol took a deep breath. "Gabriela is her name?" she whispered.

"Perhaps you will have a talk with your son." Teresa hung up.

Carol fumbled the phone, then slammed it sharply into its cradle. She had no heart to call Laurence. She'd known Finn was out walking at night. She knew he kept part of himself private—like where and when he had lunch, and how much he had to attend his classes in order to graduate. She considered his growing privacy to be normal for a teenage son. But Carol had no idea who Gabriela really was—friend, girlfriend, more? He'd mentioned sitting in on a mariachi band, but performing? Why would Finn be so secretive, when he knew she'd approve?

She dialed Laurence's number after all and did her best to recount the phone call. "Take me with you, to the next mariachi performance," said Laurence. "They have a good reputation. Wonderful they have Finn playing with them. I can't wait."

Carol could see him in his chair, an impish smile on his face. "I'm not calling to invite you somewhere. You *know* that. I don't know when they perform. I know nothing."

"That's the heck of it," said Laurence, all trace of humor gone. "No matter your plans. No matter your intentions. No matter your desire. You never know when or if you'll get what you want. You know nothing."

"Are you talking about me, or about yourself?" asked Carol.

"Both. And neither," said Laurence. "But tell me if you're going to hear the mariachi. I'll take a cab. You can come and go unencumbered by me." Carol heard Laurence's resignation.

"Laurence, you are your own encumbrance," she said.

"Because I'm crippled?" asked Laurence.

"Because you are *content* to be crippled. I've told you. When you are no longer satisfied with the state you're in . . . unemployed . . . on disability . . . that infernal chair   maybe then we can talk."

"Did Teresa give you her last name?"

"Laurence, please. I know I'm being stubborn. I miss the rose petals. I miss *you*." Carol waited for what he would say next, but he was silent. "Laurence?"

"Carol, my heart races. Faster than my legs ever will. May I call you soon?" He hung up before she could answer.

Carol paid bills to distract herself. Then, in spite of her better judgment, she went to Finn's room. She turned on his computer. While it booted up, she took a quick look through his dresser drawers. She found nothing extraordinary. She quickly searched his computer files and found nothing puzzling, revealing, or shocking.

Since Matt Groner hadn't called, she called him. The news was good and bad. Scraps had rallied and was eating on his own. He could come home. But the tumors were swelling. "I can teach you to give the fluids and the morphine, if Scraps relapses again. Or more like *when*," he emphasized.

"And then?"

"We'll have to put Scraps to sleep," said Dr. Groner.

"I'll come right over," said Carol.

Scraps was happy to see her. *Ah*, she thought, *how I will miss this kind of loyalty.* Groner's assistant taught her emergency procedures and helped her to the car. Home, Carol waited for Finn. She could imagine his relief.

Finn called as school was letting out. "Mom," he said, "Mr. Riley wants help setting up. Hope you don't mind. He's getting us pizza if we work through. Will I see you tonight?".

"Of course you'll see me," said Carol. "I've never missed a concert. And guess who else you'll see? When you get home?"

"Scraps? Really?"

"Really," said Carol. "He's a little bit better, at least for now."

"That's great, Mom," said Finn. "Catch you soon."

"Wait, Finn—" Carol said, but Finn had hung up before she could mention Teresa. Could she trust him? Would a better mother drive straight to school and confront him with what she knew to be his lie about the day before?

He had already declared, when he applied for early graduation and won the scholarship to college, that he was ready to be his own person. When would she start allowing that? Would she drive to Minnesota if she were concerned about him? No. He was an adult, and a good adult, at that. She consoled herself with resolution: she'd go to the school early, as soon as she made a quick supper of Fezziwig leftovers, and see what she could intuit.

Finn was there when she arrived, waving to her from backstage. Mr. Riley always claimed he was lucky to have a class like Finn's; all of them had played together since they were in elementary school, all of them knew each other's strengths, all of them anticipated what they could do if they worked hard together. Carol scanned the audience. She guessed the woman Teresa might be there, but she had no idea which face, among the sea of faces—white, black, Hispanic—might match the voice she'd heard that afternoon.

Caldwell was not in the audience. Sometimes she'd not see him at a concert, then bump into him at the cookies-and-punch reception in the cafeteria after. This night, through the first half of the program, then the intermission, then a martial second half of the program—English band music from the Second World War— Carol found herself alone at the reception. No Caldwell. No Laurence, either, though Finn had mentioned the concert at the Fezziwig meal. And worse, no Finn. She went to the auditorium to see if he was putting away chairs or breaking down the risers. The huge hall was as empty and dark as Finn's secrets. She went back to the reception to chat with parents. She found several of Finn's friends and asked if they knew where he was. Mr. Riley greeted her warmly. Carol asked when he'd seen Finn last.

"I only see Finn when he wants me to see him," said Mr. Riley. "Since I wrote to you, he promised he wouldn't miss his classes, and he's kept his promise. Is everything all right?"

"I don't think I can tell you," said Carol. "Senioritis perhaps?"

"He wouldn't be the first to come down with *that* disease." Mr. Riley moved on to easier encounters: quick handshakes, back-patting, and congratulations.

Home, Carol checked for messages. None. Scraps whined from the pantry, and she went to fill his bowl and lay out some treats. Scraps looked at her with sad brown eyes. Finally, Carol took off her coat, poured herself a glass of leftover negus, and sat in the dark living room.

She sipped slowly, to let time pass, and finally she heard Finn's footsteps on the porch. She snapped from her chair. She went to the kitchen and stuck her glass in the dishwasher. She came back into the living room in time to see Finn's back heading up the stairs. "Just a minute," she said. "We need to talk."

Finn did not turn around. "Can we talk in the morning?"

Carol approached the stairs. "Where were you?"

"Didn't Riley tell you? I had to see a friend. She used to play in the band. She's sick."

"Gabriela?" Carol asked.

Finn turned.

Carol went into the living room, turned on the light, and sat down. She motioned for Finn to join her.

Reluctantly, he came down and slouched on the couch. "It's no big deal, is it?"

"When I don't know where you are, it's a big deal. When I look for you after the concert and no one knows where you are, it's a big deal. When I get a call from a Teresa saying you were with her mariachi band, and you got hit in the stomach, but you said you were with your father yesterday, it's a big deal. When you plan a trip with your father before even mentioning the possibility to me, it's a big deal. When you act like I'm a pain in the ass all this Christmas, it's a big deal. Life *is* a big deal, Finn, so don't sit there all cool and smug and know-it-all when you've been lying to me and doing things behind my back." Carol folded her arms and sat on the edge of her chair.

Finn looked tired, with dark circles around his eyes. His mouth was still red from his evening of playing the trumpet. "I'm not doing anything wrong," he said.

"Gabriela?"

"She's a friend. She used to be in band. Her father might be kicking her out of her house," said Finn. "So most nights I check on her to see if it's happened yet."

"But why didn't you tell me?" Carol threw up her hands.

Finn sat back again and stared at the ceiling. He took a deep breath and blew it out. "You're all uptight about Christmas, about everything just the way you want it. And you want me to go through the motions with you, as though your routines will make everything all right. I haven't told you stuff 'cause you don't really want to listen." Finn stood up and moved closer to her chair. "You've got this big list of things, and you're going down the list checking them off, and I'm not really on your list. Not as *me*, anyway. You're just doing your Christmas, like usual. But everything *isn't* like usual for me. And you're not even enjoying yourself this year, or you wouldn't be so focused on me. Just sit for a minute and think about what's really important and quit acting like you know everything." Finn picked up the copy of *A Christmas Carol* from the coffee table. "I hate this book," he said. "You're as bad as Scrooge in his counting house." He smacked the book down and started up the stairs.

Carol took a deep breath. She needed to cry, but she didn't want to give Finn the satisfaction. "Finn!" she yelled. She waited for him to stop on the landing. "Haven't you forgotten something? Scraps is home."

Finn shrugged his shoulders and climbed the rest of the stairs to his room.

tuesday, december 23

Carol was determined to stay calm. Finn had been hurtful. She had, too. She would trust his love for Scraps. She would let him suggest the next way to mark Christmas. She would wait. The evening would bring another concert. Then, Christmas Eve Day. Surely he'd come around by Christmas, with the promise of presents under the tree? Then, Arizona with his father. She had wished for all twelve days of Christmas with Finn, but she'd also planned her research.

Finn came downstairs and went first to Scraps. Carol heard him in the pantry, soothing his dog. After a bowl of cereal, Finn left for school, giving Carol a curt good-bye.

Although Carol had promised herself she wouldn't, she picked up the phone. She felt stupid calling Freda so soon, but when her friend answered the phone—and how likely was it that Carol would find her in her apartment?—her voice alone caused Carol to choke on a sob. She got hold of herself. She talked as fast as she could, of Scraps and Laurence and Finn and Caldwell—"the tumult of men," as they'd so frequently called it—and Freda listened without interruption. Carol was embarrassed when she heard Freda, hand barely over the phone, whisper, "Not now. Just one minute."

"Oh, you're with someone?" asked Carol.

"Nothing important," said Freda, her voice full of breath. "Nothing that can't wait until later," she said, emphasizing the *later* for the person who was so obviously in the room with her. Freda giggled. "Really, Carol, keep talking."

Carol asked for advice. Freda might have been distracted, but she was true to form: "Give Scraps a good sendoff. That's all you can do now. Laurence, don't worry. Tough love before any other love, okay? Finn? Trust him, but talk, talk, talk, so he's the one responsible for what he says or doesn't say. Caldwell? Do I have to say anything besides good riddance? But what about you? You've talked about everyone but yourself."

"Yes, me," said Carol.

"Pay attention to yourself for once, okay? Not your rituals, your *self*. Okay?"

"I know." Carol had heard the same thing before. Perhaps that's why she'd called Freda.

"Oh, and one more thing," said Freda. "Plan a pleasure trip. Even if you can't get away for a while. Plan, plan, plan. You won't believe it."

"I know you're busy," said Carol. "I'll let you go. Thanks." She hung up the phone before Freda could tell her about whatever pleasure she'd interrupted.

Carol went to the pantry to be with Scraps, massaging the dog's bony head, like Matt Groner had, in the deep spaces just above the eyes. Scraps did not whine nor wince. Carol topped the water bowl and set out a treat. "Be back in a couple, three hours, Trooper," she said. Carol forced herself toward the door before she was tempted to call Laurence. Or the school to make sure Finn was there. Or Caldwell to read him her letter. She would go to her study carrel and count semicolons. What was the Biblical injunction? *Work, for the night is coming.*

Before she implemented her research, she wanted to check in on the punctuation of some American fiction writers of the late nineteenth century. Henry James, that American who lived and wrote wholeheartedly in the British tradition, was a consistent practitioner of elegant punctuation: in his 1877 novel *The American* Carol counted thirty-six semicolons in the first chapter; in chapter one of *Washington Square*, published in 1880, she counted ten, though it was an uncharacteristically short chapter. The first chapter of James' 1904 *The Golden Bowl* contained twenty-nine semicolons.

Carol looked to American Regionalism: not a single semicolon in the whole of Hamlin Garland's "Under the Lion's Paw," one of eleven stories in his 1891 *Main-Travelled Roads*. Mark Twain used twenty-three semicolons in the very short first two chapters of the 1881 *The Prince and the Pauper.* Thirteen years later, in the first chapter of *The Tragedy of Pudd'nhead Wilson and the Comedy of Those Extraordinary Twins*, Twain continued to rely on the semicolon, using seventeen.

American literature always muddied Carol's theories. Was it the eclectic, democratic, erratic, class-breaking nature of American culture that made everything from punctuation to politics so unpredictable? She would abandon the American fiction, focus on her new plan after Christmas. Then she'd have to write the paper she'd proposed for the spring conference.

She'd make a different Twelve Days of Christmas without Finn. They'd always sung the song; they'd made little jokes together. Once, on the Third Day of Christmas, Finn placed three French horns in the living room. Sitting in her study carrel, her morning's work finished, Carol Dickens remembered her London

Christmas, when she'd recovered Christmas as her own holiday. She had stood in front of the Charles Dickens House. She'd seen it so many times—sketched, photographed, described—she felt she was standing in front of a picture. The house was real, though, the air damp and cold. She was surrounded by others on the sidewalk, the street, the occupied buildings. The young Finn stood at her side. For one moment she saw herself as though in a picture; at the same time, she was looking at the picture.

Carol stacked her books and grabbed her purse. Work was no good—studying the past, visiting the past. What had she felt in front of Dickens' house? Reverence? Or had it been regret: she was so enamored of the past that she was compelled to search it out?

Carol left the library. The past would not salvage the future. Finnegan Dickens-Dunmore could not hold the key to her Christmas either. Carol drove to the grocery store. Already she'd waited too long to find the biggest turkey, one that "never could have stood upon his legs," that "would have snapped 'em short off in a minute, like sticks of sealing-wax." To her surprise she found just such a bird, twenty-six pounds of extravagance and good cheer. For contrast she would serve Cornish hens alongside the massive turkey; she put two in her shopping cart. She bought six firm, unblemished russet potatoes to mash. And ground pork sausage to put in the dressing, and two loaves of white bread to dry, and a chicken to boil for broth, and sweet potatoes to bake and cover with caramelized onions, and fresh green beans and beets, and tins of oysters, and oranges and apples, and mixed nuts and olives, and packed pumpkin and pecans for pies. Surrounded by groceries, in her car again, she felt centered and focused—let Finn and Laurence and Caldwell and everyone else be damned. She stopped at the liquor store. She was out of Nutcracker Ale, and Beaujolais Nouveau and a good

Chardonnay would complement the meal. As would Grand Marnier, that wonderful mixture of cognac and orange that had taken the world by storm after its creation in 1880, when people still used semicolons regularly in their writing. Carol liked the idea of finishing a meal with something old and expensive. And, looking ahead to her traditional meal on January sixth, Epiphany, she bought two bottles of cheap red wine and a bottle of ruby port for her version of Smoking Bishop. She winced at the cash register, but this was *her* Christmas, perhaps hers alone. Maybe she *did* have her list, as Finn had said, and maybe she *was* slave to her routines.

But maybe she was just being herself, for herself. Exactly as Freda, probably still in bed with that someone, had suggested. She was being the only way she could be. She couldn't wait to get home, fill her cabinets and refrigerator, and sit in a house made richer by the promise of food and spirits.

After his mother's accusations, and his nastiness to her, Finn expected the worst. She knew about Gabriela and Teresa, and she'd be watching him closely. She'd be hurt, of course, as she always was when he argued with her. She'd use Scraps against him, after all he'd done to keep his childhood companion alive. She'd start calling everyone to check up on him, too. School office, Mr. Riley. Would she call his father?

But she had let him go to school without a confrontation, and she seemed cheerful when he got home. They had a quiet dinner before the jazz band swing night, a meatloaf and salad, "For old times' sake," Carol said.

"What do you mean?" he asked her.

"When you were little, the only meat you'd eat was my meatloaf. I made it with Quaker oats, catsup, milk, and egg. Nothing else."

"And that's what's in here?" asked Finn.

Carol nodded.

"Needs some salt," he said and grinned.

After dinner they went to their rooms to dress for the concert. Carol came out in the same dress she wore every year. "So I can really swing," she said. Finn shook his head.

The jazz band swing night was Mr. Riley's idea of fun. Instead of performing on a stage, the kids turned the cafeteria into the kind of dance hall usually created for them at the small-town middle and high schools where they played during the year. Instead of sitting, quietly listening, parents and friends found partners. After some hesitancy—in the adults as well as high school kids—most everyone danced. Freshman year, Finn wondered if Carol would go by herself and end up asking some married guy to dance. Instead, at the last minute she'd invited Laurence Timmons, and they'd danced enough to participate, not enough to be a center of attention.

Finn was not relieved when Laurence wheeled into the cafeteria this evening. Carol hadn't said he was coming. You wouldn't invite a guy in a wheelchair to a dance. During the first number Finn looked out at the dance floor and saw Teresa, dressed in a flouncing sequined skirt, dancing with someone. In the muted light Finn thought for an instant the man might be Gabriela's father. Worried, he missed a cue. Mr. Riley stared him down.

After intermission, during a slow number Finn knew by heart, Carol pulled Laurence onto the dance floor. Not everyone had begun dancing again, and Laurence's wheelchair was conspicuous. Carol stood in front of Laurence and shifted her weight from side to side. Laurence moved first one wheel, then the next, forward slightly, then back. He moved his head to the beat, and occasionally raised one arm, then the other, from the wheels of his chair. At first Finn felt embarrassed. But Laurence's smooth movements and abandoned smile forced Finn to forget what people might think. Laurence was "feeling the music," something Mr. Riley always cajoled his students to do. Finn watched, amused, until Teresa tapped his mother on the shoulder and cut in. Carol nodded and found a seat at the edge of the room.

Maybe Finn was tired from staying up late the night before. Maybe it was the heat in the cafeteria, with all the bodies dancing, the school furnace turned up too high. Maybe he was seeing things. But he thought he saw Mr. Marble come in the door and take a seat in the back. Soon after, Gabriela and her father arrived. Had Mr. Marble dragged them here, or had they dragged Mr. Marble? Then Caldwell Dunmore walked into the cafeteria, found Finn's mother, and asked her to dance. They were talking, too. Finn was in a nightmare. His tangled relationships, each separate, looked as though they might weave together. The jazz band began their last number; Finn began to sweat. He debated running from the room. As the band held the last wavering note of the last song of the evening, Finn closed his eyes, and Scraps leaned his head onto Finn's shoulder and whimpered, his wet fur brushing Finn's ear, his eyes full of unshed tears. The sensation was so real Finn almost wept. When the last note faded into applause, Finn woke from his reverie. The lights were bright again. He stood up and waved at his mother, at Laurence, at Teresa, at Gabriela and her father, at Mr. Marble, at his father. Finn set his horn on his chair and walked onto the floor.

He went to Laurence first. "You were cool out there," he said.

Laurence held out his arm. "You guys were great."

Finn turned to the group gathering around him. "Mom," he said and gave her a hug.

"This was fun," she said. "Especially the swinging Christmas numbers."

"We play them every year," said Finn.

"They were sweetest for your last swing night," she said, but Finn was already turning her by the elbow to where Gabriela stood with her father and her aunt.

"Mom, meet my newest music teacher. Teresa, this is my mom, Carol Dickens." He almost pushed his mother toward the mariachi bandleader.

Carol took Teresa's hand. "Nice to meet you in person," she said.

"*Mucho gusto*," said Teresa. "Finn plays so well."

"Thank you for calling me," Carol said. "I'm happy Finn is playing with you. Even if he *is* going off to college. He *has* told you? Macalester, to study music. He's leaving mid-January."

Teresa nodded. "And he will take some of our music with him. You've met our Gabriela?" Finn was relieved to have Teresa do the introduction, though he wondered what his mother thought of his friend, large as she was, larger than he remembered in the dress she wore. "And her father, Roberto," said Teresa. "He was once a fine horn player himself."

Carol briefly took Gabriela's hand, smiling. She simply nodded at Roberto. "And Mr. Marble." She turned to the chimney sweep for rescue. "How nice of you to come."

"I sweep, but I am also swept," said the old man, taking off his hat and making a formal bow, "by such music." He took Finn's hand. "A steady hand. And steady lips, my boy," he observed. "For years I've heard you practice that horn as I raided the carriage house for supplies. But I've never heard you perform. I've waited long enough, I told myself. Read about you in the paper, I did, and here I am."

Finn let go of Mr. Marble's hand. His father waited at the edge of their small circle. Finn wasn't sure what to say, but Mr. Marble brought Finn's father into their circle with a handshake. "Caldwell

Dunmore, we meet again," said the chimney sweep. "Progenitor of this fine young man. Supporter, too. How nice to see you."

Caldwell smiled. He let go of Mr. Marble's hand and took Finn's. "Good job, Son," he said. "Glad I could finally make it to one of your programs. Been very busy. Too busy."

"That's why they call it busy-ness, am I right?" asked Mr. Marble.

"Glad you could come, Dad," Finn said. "We'll have plenty of time to visit. After Christmas, huh?"

Carol winced.

Laurence moved his chair forward. "Caldwell," he said, "I don't believe we've seen each other since my accident. My *reduced circumstances*, as I call them." Laurence held his hand up as though to measure his height, to show himself only as tall in his chair as Caldwell's chest.

"I was sorry to hear, you know that," said Caldwell.

"Indeed," said Laurence. He turned to Finn. "Don't you want some refreshments? Some punch? You must be thirsty, and all your admirers are keeping you from the treats. And from your friends. Away," said Laurence, "to the cookies." He shooed Finn from the circle of odd possibilities—of who might say what next, and what it would mean to Finn and his plans.

Finn headed for refreshments feeling suddenly light, as though he'd walked through a minefield and survived. He found a peanut-butter cookie full of peanut M&M's. Mr. Riley's wife baked dozens of them each year for after-concert parties. He stacked three of them on a napkin and poured himself some punch. He had survived swing night.

Home again, Finn checked on Scraps. The old dog lifted his head and sighed. "Scraps, Scraps, Scraps," Finn sang. Carol joined him, but he soon pleaded exhaustion and headed to his room before she could grill him.

wednesday, december 24

Christmas Eve day, up early to check on Scraps, then unable to go back to sleep, Finn sat in his bedroom chair, looking out the window. On this cold, windy morning all the leaves he'd refused to rake for the past three weeks bounced and scuttled through the yard, made patterns and shapes, then dissipated. Finn considered them. He found faces in them, frowns and grimaces, crossed eyes, cyclopean monstrosities. Then they were leaves again, random and nothing. Once, he'd felt exactly like them, sometimes shaped and sometimes blown by the wind. He remembered a time when his father wouldn't let him do anything until he'd raked leaves. He was eleven years old. "Rake, or you'll stay in your room doing nothing," his father had said. Finn had sat in his room for hours, looking at the leaves. Later that fall his dad walked out. Back then he'd felt sorry for himself. Now he felt sorry for the boy he'd once been. The limbs of the huge ash tree shook in the wind, bare and pretending death for the winter. He looked to the highest branches, the ones most flexible, even in the harsh cold. All these years, he'd been thinking of himself as a leaf, blown by winds he couldn't control. Why leaf instead of tree? If he were the tree, then the leaves would be *his* to give up. He went downstairs and headed for the door.

"Where are you going?" asked his mother from the kitchen.

"To rake my leaves," he said and shrugged his shoulders. He didn't wait to see the smile on her face. She thought she'd won. Let her.

Having seen both Laurence and Mr. Marble the night before, Carol remembered how much Laurence had always liked a good fire. She bet he had not built a fire since the accident. She added a gift idea to her list. Mr. Marble would go to Laurence's house soon after Christmas, sweep his chimney, and build a fire. He'd deliver a little gift, as well. With Finn raking leaves, she sat down to finish planning the Christmas meal. She felt right in trusting Finn. Gabriela was a waifish girl, tired, with smudged eyes. She was thin, even with her huge womb. She'd have her child, and Finn would leave for college, and the girl would make peace with her uncomfortable father—and whatever other family she had— as most teenage girls eventually did after the birth of a baby out of wedlock. People tended to respond better to the helplessness of an infant than to the helplessness of a child giving birth to one. Finn *should* go with his father; perhaps he'd even embraced the Arizona plan to get away from the Gabriela situation. Could Scraps hold on through Finn's week away? Would Finn be all right with a decision to put the dog down, if Matt Groner said Scraps' time had come? She'd talk to Finn when he finished with his leaves.

Carol registered quiet and looked out the window; the rake was propped against the carriage house next to two large trash cans. Mr. Marble's truck nudged its way quietly down the alley, Finn in the passenger seat. When Carol called Mr. Marble about

Laurence's fireplace, she'd ask what he was doing with her son on Christmas Eve. She'd put that on her list, too. She started to her desk for a pad and pencil, then stopped herself.

Finn had told her she was too busy making lists, checking them off. Why didn't she just take care of herself, as Freda had told her? And *herself* also included her rituals. Carol wanted a lovely Christmas dinner. She'd prepare one. She took the huge turkey out of the refrigerator to finish thawing in cold water. By evening she'd have it stuffed, ready to put in the oven—as was her method—in the middle of the night. The Cornish hens were already thawed enough to stuff and cook. She put oysters in chicken broth, let them simmer, then strained them out. She melted butter, added flour to make a paste, then added cream and broth a little at a time, whisking everything together until the thick liquid oozed off the whisk. She added lemon peel, salt, cracked pepper, and the oysters, and adjusted it for consistency. She took many small tastes as she cooked: anticipation creates keen appetite.

She hadn't yet invited Laurence. Would that create appetite, as well? She went to the phone. When he answered, she spoke like an announcer: "The presence of your company is requested on Christmas Day at the home of Carol Dickens, who will be disappointed if you can't come. But beyond that, you will be disappointed at what you'll miss, for I am even now in the midst of creating a banquet sure to remain in your memory for years to come."

"And at what time might I haul my presence over there?"

"Two o'clock sharp," said Carol.

"Delighted," said Laurence and hung up.

Carol pulled the chicken from the refrigerator, took it from its plastic, and removed the small paper bag of giblets; she'd bought the cheapest chicken she could because some of the fancier labels had stupidly dispensed with giblets altogether. Most people did not want to be bothered with gizzard, liver, heart, and neck. Carol would have missed their flavor. She put them in a pot of hot water and cut the chicken into parts to simmer. By the time she strained the liquid, with its thick fat and golden broth, the meat would have given up its flavor. The Christmas before, she would have fed the threaded meat to Scraps.

Carol stopped herself from thinking about the dog. Gravy and not grave, to borrow from Dickens, was what she wanted. She put half a cup of water on the stove to boil, added a third of a cup of white balsamic vinegar, a fourth of a cup of brown sugar, a half dozen shakes of salt, a dozen shakes of pepper, a teaspoon of dried dill, and three allspice seeds. She brought the mixture to a boil, then turned it down to simmer. She washed and snapped the green beans, put them in her steamer, and cooked them until they were just tender—still bright green, no touch of gray. She laid them in a cake pan, because she had a plastic lid for it, and poured on the hot dill sauce. The anticipation of their flavor the next day was as powerful as the anticipation of the oyster sauce.

Carol took the loaves of white bread from their plastic wrap and broke the bread into small pieces in a large bowl. She put the beets on to boil. She'd pickle them with cinnamon and cloves, nutmeg and garlic—a whole head of garlic to balance the sweetness of the beets, to deepen the fruity spices. She would bake the pies that evening; a day-old pie was often more flavorful than one hot from the oven. Surrounded by the smells of accomplishment—a bit of yeast on her fingers from the bread, the sharp dill and vinegar in her nostrils, the rich rendering of the chicken that would soon almost cloy the house— Carol felt satisfied.

Finn came in the front door, letting the storm door bang after him. He went upstairs without greeting Carol. She climbed the stairs. "Did you have a good time with Mr. Marble?" she asked his closed door. When he didn't answer, she knocked.

"Come in," he said.

Finn lay on his bed, staring at the ceiling. "Did you have a nice time with Mr. Marble?" Carol asked again. "Did you invite him to Christmas dinner. Can you smell it?"

Finn sat up. "I forgot," he said.

"You could invite your friend Gabriela," said Carol. "We'll have plenty to eat, and she doesn't look sick. She's eating for two, in fact."

Finn studied her as though trying to find sarcasm in her voice. "Actually, she says she's not hungry these days."

"Really?" asked Carol.

"Is that normal?" asked Finn. "I mean, were you hungry before you had me?"

Carol sat on the edge of Finn's bed. As though to bring back the memory, she put her hands over her stomach. "I was ravenous," she said. "I loved being pregnant. You were so big, you didn't give my stomach much room. So I ate a little bit a lot of the time. I ate continuously. And I was eating for you, so my pleasure was doubled."

"Gabriela's too nervous to eat much," said Finn.

Carol touched his knee. He let her hand rest there.

"Her father's really on her case. Not last night. But when nobody's around. It's like the closer she gets to having the baby, and the bigger she gets, the madder he is."

"And you need to rescue her?"

Finn jerked his knee from under her palm. "I walked by their house one night. We had lunch the next day. Then we started hanging out."

"So you don't have anything to do with her . . . condition?" asked Carol.

"You can say pregnant, Mom," said Finn. He looked at the ceiling.

Carol put her hand under his chin, forcing him to look at her.

"You know I don't," said Finn.

"Are you in over your head?"

"No," said Finn.

"I've been trying not to confront you," said Carol. "About Scraps, about your being gone so much, about planning a trip with your father, about Gabriela, about the mariachi band. All these surprises, Finn. Can't we just keep Christmas?"

"We are, aren't we?"

"We are. And there's nothing wrong with that. Traditions keep us going. They make things meaningful."

Finn stared at the ceiling. "Like school? You do the same things at the same time year after year until you can't stand it anymore."

"Is that how you feel about our Christmas?"

"Nothing stopped Dad from leaving," said Finn. "That was a holiday, remember? Now Scraps is dying, and it's a holiday. Dad was ready to kick Gabriela's family out of her house, and it was Christmas, for Christ's sake."

"He was their landlord?" asked Carol.

Finn scooted off the bed. "Traditions might make you feel good, but they don't change what happens." He started out the door.

Carol stood up. "Where are you going?" she said.

Finn stopped in the hall. "Nothing's going to stop me from leaving, either!" he shouted.

"Oh, Finn," said Carol. "I'm not trying to stop you from doing anything." She wanted to hug him, but she imagined him squirming away, heading down the stairs and out the door. "Finn," she said. "Please. I just want to help you."

For one moment Finn looked like he might bend, might include her in whatever was happening in his life; he leaned forward and Carol saw him as he might appear when he was an old man, trying to listen to a conversation that did not include him. She suddenly felt older herself, with her graying hair, the crow's feet at the edges of her eyes. She squinted, as though to focus better on Finn.

"You want *me* to help *you*," said Finn. "To get through Christmas. Mom, Gabriela actually needs me. Do you understand?"

"I shouldn't need you?" asked Carol.

"You shouldn't need anyone," Finn said. He wouldn't look at her.

"Everybody needs people. No matter how old they are. Or young," said Carol.

"But Gabriela *really* needs me. Maybe more than you, if you can believe it. Maybe more than Scraps. Maybe more than anything else. I've got to go to a mariachi practice, okay?" He started down the stairs.

"On Christmas Eve?" Carol asked.

Finn stopped at the bottom of the stairs. "Special rehearsal. We're going to perform after New Year's. You're going to be invited."

"Traditional music," Carol said. She folded her arms over her chest and sighed. "Traditions must not be all bad."

"I'll invite Gabriela to Christmas dinner, but I don't think she'll come."

"If she could smell this house," said Carol, "she'd get her appetite back."

Finn rolled his eyes. "You cook some pretty weird stuff."

"Traditional weird stuff," said Carol.

"Yeah," said Finn. "See you later." He was out the door before Carol could ask what he planned to eat for lunch.

Carol went to her bedroom window and looked at him in nothing but a hooded sweatshirt and gloves, though cold was settling in. He was halfway down the street already, ambling toward wherever. He didn't have his trumpet with him. *Mariachi, indeed*, she thought.

She went to her closet. In the back she found the two big gifts for Finn's Christmas morning. Presents for the future: a set of luggage, carry-on size, as well as a briefcase; and a new trumpet, a silver Bach. Oh, the tone Finn would accomplish on such a horn, though he'd accomplish it in Minnesota.

Suddenly hungry, Carol went to the kitchen. From the pantry Scraps raised his head, almost caved in he had become so thin. He rested it between his large paws. Carol wished she'd saved the tamales she'd thrown away, day after day, without telling Finn that his dog had no appetite for them.

Carol bundled up and hurried to Rosaria's, not sure whether the restaurant would be open Christmas Eve. The sign on the door announced a two o'clock closing; Carol's watch said one fifty-five. She pushed in. A few diners sat at tables. Rosaria came out from the kitchen and waved Carol to a seat. Carol pointed to her watch. "To go," she said. "Tamales, please."

Rosaria came to her. "You can stay past closing. So many people today want to take their food with them. We sell so many tamales, but visit with so few people."

"Thanks," said Carol, "but my son might be home any time. I need to be there."

"How many tamales?" asked Rosaria. She pulled a chair from a table so Carol could sit while she waited.

"Three chicken," said Carol. "Oh, and one dessert. You still sell those during Christmas? My son loves them."

Rosaria nodded and went to the kitchen. Carol sat. She hadn't been in the restaurant for several years. All was as she remembered, including the old man who sat in the corner. Carol fumbled for his name.

As though he could read her thoughts, the old man shifted in his chair. "I am Juan."

Carol stood up and approached him. "You are Rosaria's father," she said. A cup in front of the old man was stuffed with dollar bills. Was it charity? Christmas was the season of giving. She took a dollar bill from her purse and put it in the old man's cup.

"God bless you," said Juan. "What is your name?"

"Carol Dickens," said Carol.

"You are right to be going home," Juan whispered. "Your Finn is not here. You are looking for him where he has been, but not where he is or where he will be."

"Do you know my son?" asked Carol.

"Finn eats here with Gabriela. She is my goddaughter. He is her friend."

"Do you know where he is right now?"

"Like you, I wonder. Gabriela will soon have her baby. Perhaps we will know where our children are only when they want us to know. The child leaves the mother's womb only when it is ready."

"Finn's leaving," said Carol. She felt silly talking to Juan, confessing her son's plans.

"Your tamales," said Rosaria, rustling a bag behind Carol.

Carol turned from Juan and went to the register. She opened her purse.

"No," said Rosaria. "Finn's mother doesn't pay today. It is Christmas Eve."

"Tell me what you know," Carol said, loud enough so Juan would know she spoke to him, too.

Juan leaned forward. "When I know anything about Finn, I will tell you," he said.

"You have a good son." Rosaria accompanied Carol to the door. "My father," she whispered, "he doesn't really know everything, he just pretends to."

"Thanks," Carol said, then hurried out the door.

Finn was not at home. Carol husked a chicken tamal for Scraps and was surprised to see the dog raise its nose and scuttle its lumpy body toward the rich smell. *The pleasure of appetite is an amazing thing*, Carol thought as she watched Scraps lick the tamal. Carol went to the table. In spite of her resolution to save one for Finn, she wolfed down the two remaining chicken and the dessert tamales before she returned to her cooking.

Finn headed through the cold toward the Birth Center. A large Victorian brick house with rounded walls, renovated into a birthing clinic, the center had escaped Finn's notice all of his growing up, but it stood less than a half mile from his house, on the corner of Sixth and Washburn. The practical Mr. Marble had suggested that they needed "a place at the inn," somewhere ready to take care of mother and baby when the time arrived. He'd promised to bring Gabriela there. Caldwell Dunmore, who was paying for some of Gabriela's medical care—anything above the amount she'd set aside in the savings account she'd started with her flower shop money—would also be there. Over lunch one day Finn had blackmailed (more like *gray*mailed) his father. He wasn't above suggesting that his father's selling of Gabriela's house had been disruptive. And, of course, he'd appealed to Caldwell's pride in being flush, in having money when Carol didn't. And Finn knew his father wanted to be involved whenever his mother hadn't been asked: they still one-upped each other, given the chance. Finn didn't mind playing his father against his mother for Gabriela's sake.

Caldwell had become more generous with Finn each year, larger allowances to cover what he called "a young man's expenses." And this year, when they got together to "do Christmas" early, Finn was generous, too. He gave his father a travel kit— something to carry toothbrush, toothpaste, razor, and other toiletries. He'd also found an Arizona road atlas, with detailed maps of every county, and exhaustive city maps, as well. He'd bought a leather folder to hold it.

Then his father presented Finn with his secret dream: Finn opened a large box to find a trumpet case. Inside that was a silver Bach, the best trumpet Finn could imagine. "I want you to excel at Macalester," his father had told him. Finn cradled the horn like a baby. "Play it," his father said.

Finn warmed the mouthpiece and put it in the horn. He blew through the trumpet to warm it, as well. The valves were soft, easy to press down, but quick to find his fingers again. Finn put the horn to his lips and blew, first mellow, then brassy. He pinched out some high notes, then let his lips loosen to mid-range vibrato and finally to an airy bottom note, sliding down and back up again. The Bach responded as though it knew exactly what he wanted from it. Finn felt at the beginning of an important partnership. "This is amazing, Dad," he said.

"I remember you talking about it from a long time back. And I know your mother doesn't always have the resources to buy you everything you want." Finn's father patted the trumpet case. "A pretty penny, that instrument. The case is the best, too."

"Thanks," said Finn. "And thanks for helping with my friend, too."

"You know I like to be there when your mother can't be," said his father.

Finn hadn't been able to take the horn home or talk about the gift to Carol. She didn't need anything more to bum her out this Christmas. Nothing was going as usual. Finn knew he'd been resistant, but he wanted things to be different. His mother could treat him like an adult, for one thing, instead of assuming he'd be a cheerleader for Dickens, Seuss, the Bible, Clement Moore, and everyone else who'd written a word about the holiday.

Finn had taken the silver Bach to Teresa's house. She'd agreed to keep it for him for rehearsals and performances. "With a gift comes responsibility. I hope for you to play it well."

"I will do my best," said Finn.

"You seem like that kind of boy," said Teresa. "With responsibility comes a gift. You have been a gift to Gabriela. To us. I will see you soon, for the appointment?"

Now Finn knocked on the door of the Birth Center. When nobody answered, he pounded until his blue hands hurt. He was ready to knock again when the door opened and a thin woman in a denim shirt and blue jeans stood before him. "You don't have to knock, we're open. In fact, we're rather busy." She tossed her head, and her long braid flipped over her shoulder. "Is it Finn?" she asked. She put out her hand. Finn touched it, and then she led him down a hall. "I'm Dr. Drewland. We've been waiting." She hurried into the first room. Finn saw some gray in her hair, though she hadn't looked old.

"That's right," came Mr. Marble's voice. "I told them we'd not proceed forward one second before our Mr. Finn arrived." Mr. Marble sat on the edge of a couch, leaning forward. Gabriela sat next to Marble, at an angle, her womb so large it needed a space all to itself. Finn's father sat as far from them as he could, in a small wooden chair in the corner.

"Let's begin, then," said Dr. Drewland. A young woman, dressed in slacks and a hospital shirt, came in from the hall. "Maria will be helping through your labor and delivery."

Maria sat next to Gabriela. "I know your brother," she said.

"Antonio?" asked Gabriela.

"You have others?" asked Maria.

"Two others," said Gabriela. "In Mexico, but they're coming soon. Maybe they're here already."

"They know about your pregnancy?" asked Maria.

Gabriela's brown skin darkened. "Everyone knows," she said. She put her chin to her chest. Her breasts had become large, one of the many changes of the past several weeks.

"We'll ask you questions when we examine you, Gabriela," said Dr. Drewland, but she was looking at Maria.

Gabriela heaved herself off the couch. "You're kind," she said. She followed Dr. Drewland and Maria into a room off what had once been the living room of the house.

A young man, clipboard in one hand, pen in the other, came into the waiting room. Down the hall, a woman screamed. "Oh, God, no, no, no, no!" Finn shifted in his chair. Lower voices from down the hall intoned patience. "Breathe," one said. "You're fine," said another. "That's fine, let it out," said the first.

"We'll be having another baby soon," said the young man. "I'm Mark Stallbaum. And you all?" He looked around the room, waiting for anyone to answer him.

"Finn," said Finn. The woman down the hall screamed again. Finn flinched with the pain of imagined childbirth.

"And?" The young man looked at Mr. Marble.

"Harry Marble. Here to support the boy, you see." He stood up to pace. "And you should meet our Mr. Dunmore." Marble pointed to the corner. Finn's father looked miserable, as though relegated to the corner by a teacher for some infraction.

"Caldwell Dunmore. I'll be paying the bill, if that's what you're after." He reached into his coat pocket and pulled out a checkbook.

"I'm after paperwork more than money, Mr. Dunmore," said Mark. He consulted his clipboard. "Though we can start there if you'd like. I have a form for you to fill out as the financially responsible party. The young woman is your daughter?"

"No," said Finn's father.

Mark turned to Finn. "You are the father of the young woman's child?"

"No," said Finn.

Mr. Marble stopped pacing. "You'd best quit asking questions, my friend," he said. "For it's a tangled situation. A jumble of string, and best not straightened out by tightening, you see. I clean this fireplace here. And the chimney, once a year, from the roof down. Last time I was here I heard a woman in labor, from clear up top. So I know your Birth Center, and I've brought my friend Finn. And his friend Gabriela. And let's just say that Mr. Caldwell Dunmore is a friend, as well. Keep things simple. We're all friends, no relation to the mother or her baby. But friends is friends." He looked at his watch. "Family will be here soon."

Mark smiled. "Nobody has attended childbirth classes with Ms. . . ." He waited for someone to tell him Gabriela's last name.

"Diaz," said Finn.

"That's right, Diaz," said Caldwell. "Her father used to rent a house from me."

"My house now," said Mr. Marble, "but soon to be his own. He has a lease to buy."

From down the hall, they heard moaning, then a spasm of groans and grunts.

Mark stuck to his paperwork. "Okay, no childbirth education classes. Prenatal care?" Nobody answered. "Do we have a due date?" Silence again, and the young man shuffled the papers on his clipboard. "Perhaps I'll have you fill out the financial paperwork?" He handed a sheet to Finn's father. "We'll find out more when Doctor returns."

Caldwell filled out the forms while the woman in labor burst with intensity: tears, then moaning, then loud screams and sighs. Finn's father took out his checkbook again. "Listen," he said to Mark, "I have an appointment. Since I'm involved only with the money side of it, here's a check. I'm signing it and making it out to you. Send me the invoice, marked paid. All this other stuff, you don't really need to know it." He finished writing the check with a flourish of signature, stood up, handed everything to Mark, and left. The silence of his departure was soon filled by the woman in labor.

Dr. Drewland stuck her head in the door. "I'm needed, as you can hear. Gabriela will be out soon."

Teresa came in first.

"And who are you?" asked Mark.

"Gabriela's aunt, Teresa," she said. "I'll be with her for the birth."

Gabriela and Maria came back into the room. Gabriela ran to Teresa. "Tía." She hugged her aunt. "You are alone?" she whispered.

"*Sí, solo.*"

Finn was happy his father had left. Although he was helping, Caldwell's heart was several sizes too small. Finn had worked hard to make sure Gabriela was safe from her father's wrath, safe from judgment and scorn. Gabriela's *abuela* should have been included. And maybe his own mother, but he couldn't worry about everyone. The others, Roberto Diaz and the brothers from Mexico who frightened Gabriela, the parish priest who wanted her to confess the identity of the father of her child, didn't understand how simple their acceptance should be: Gabriela was daughter, sister, parishioner.

In the room down the hall the raucous noise stopped. Finn waited. A baby cried, powerful lungs breathing air, vocal chords giving their first sounds to a world open to whatever might be expressed. A moment later, Dr. Drewland stuck her head in the door. "A girl," she said, and gave a thumbs up. "Maria, we need you."

Maria left the room. A loud knocking came from the front door. Finn went to open it. In the doorway stood Juan. Finn wasn't certain what to say. "My Gabriela, she is here?" asked the old man.

"I'll take you," said Finn.

"Ah, it is Finn," said Juan. "She is with her *tía*?"

"She is," said Finn.

Juan hand found Finn's arm. "Listen." He stayed in the entryway. "Roberto wonders where Gabriela is. In the restaurant, with his sons, he makes plans to take her to Mexico, to have the baby there. The church in their village will see it taken from her and adopted."

"Does he know she is here?" asked Finn.

"He looks for her," said the old man. "If he finds her, you will not see her again."

"How did you know where we were?" asked Finn.

"I was to wait in Teresa's car. But do you know how loud all of you are?" Juan asked. Down the hall the baby began to squall again. Juan smiled. "So loud," he said. "Take Gabriela somewhere safe. Not to your house. Roberto will go there sometime today. He will speak to your mother. She is looking for you. She, too, came to Rosaria's. I spoke with her. So many parents looking for children. When Rosaria called Teresa, and she told us where to find you, I wanted to come."

Finn's heart pounded. "We should tell Gabriela and Teresa," said Finn.

"I have said what I know. I must leave. I cannot see, but also I must not be seen." He pulled his large hat down over his head and tapped his way out the door.

Finn ran to the others to explain what Juan had told him. Mr. Marble jumped toward the door. "I'll take Juan home, Teresa. Then I'll find Roberto. Talk some sense. Surely a landlord has a little power."

"I will go to your mother," said Teresa to Finn. He gave her the address.

Looking from Finn to Gabriela, Mark said, "I could drive you two somewhere, if you have a place to go."

"You can't tell anyone," said Finn.

"I'm used to keeping secrets," said Mark. "If you only knew how many." He looked at his clipboard again. "I don't have Gabriela's age. I assume she's not eighteen?"

Both Finn and Gabriela shook their heads.

"Then you have to keep a secret, too. I didn't help you." He set the clipboard down and reached into his pocket for his keys.

From the back seat, Finn gave Mark directions through side streets and alleys. He held Gabriela's cold hand in his warm one. His other hand was in his pocket, fingering a key.

By late afternoon, Carol was worried. Whatever calm she'd felt after talking to Juan and Rosaria, after cooking all afternoon and anticipating a wonderful Christmas, after telling herself to trust Finn—that calm had dissipated. She was as gloomy as the lowering sky. Carol kept pacing to the front window. She poured herself a glass of wine and put on a CD Finn had given her when he was too young to know any better, maybe nine or ten. She'd told him the story of the awful Christmas when her father was so drunk he couldn't wake up. She'd mentioned her father's favorite Christmas music, and Finn had convinced Caldwell to buy *A Frank Sinatra Christmas*. Carol had played it once, to please Finn, then resolved never to listen to it again. Her father's generation had revered the mellow, nonchalant sound of singers like Bing Crosby and Frank Sinatra. When Carol heard their version of the classics, the "Have Yourself a Merry Little Christmas," she was cloyed by their worldly condescension, by the way Sinatra claimed to hear the "Bells on Christmas Day, their old, familiar carols play" when it was he, himself, who wanted to be familiar. And rich. *That was it*, Carol thought. Sinatra sounded both world weary and wealthy, which, of course, he was. But Carol liked "The Little Drummer Boy" and "The Twelve Days of Christmas" no matter who sang them, so, as the years passed she played the Sinatra CD once a season.

Carol was startled by a banging on the door. A short man with a wispy beard, a black stocking cap almost covering his eyes, stood on her front porch, his arms crossed over his chest. Carol thought she recognized Gabriela's father from the swing night, so she turned on the porch light against the graying day. Roberto looked decidedly unhappy in his grimy jacket. Carol turned off the light, mad at herself for letting him know she was home. No law said she had to answer the door. The man banged again. She'd give him five minutes before she called the police. He sat on the porch swing for a moment. From the hall, where she could watch from shadow, Carol saw him get up and look in the window. He rapped on the plate glass until it shook. "Hello! Hello!" he yelled. She went into the kitchen for the phone, but just as she pressed the nine she heard the man's footsteps on the porch stairs. She came into the living room and looked out the narrow window at the top of the front door. A car sped away.

Ten minutes later, just as her heart quieted its pounding, Carol heard another knock. She stayed in her chair. The day had given itself over to a foggy mist. Carol had not yet turned on any lights. Nobody could see in, but she could see out. Teresa, Gabriela's aunt, paced the porch, knocked again, and left. Perhaps she should have answered. This woman had Finn's best interests in mind. Or did she? Did anyone? Certainly this infatuation with Gabriela had turned Finn moody, touchy, distant. Certainly Finn didn't need to learn mariachi when he was moving away so soon. Certainly Finn had neglected Christmas, along with Carol and Scraps. Certainly Caldwell was taking advantage of Finn's transition to take him away for a week, when Carol only had Finn under her roof for three more weeks. Certainly Gabriela would do nothing to make Finn's leaving any easier.

The phone rang. "Have you heard?" Laurence's voice asked. "Heard what?"

"Winter storm advisory," said Laurence. "Turn on the television. Ice everywhere. Already there's no power in Abilene. Trees are snapping. Lines are down. It'll be here soon."

Carol put down the phone and looked out the dining room window. Small bits of ice flicked at the glass. She came back. "I don't know where Finn is."

"Can I come over?" asked Laurence. "Before things hit hard? I'll get a cab. I'd be helpful."

"You don't want to be home alone, do you?" asked Carol.

"You don't believe I can be of use?" Laurence asked.

Carol did not want a prolonged conversation. Finn might be trying to call.

"Maybe I *can't* be of use," said Laurence. "Once you replaced yourself with Mrs. Cross, I lost one more reason to be hopeful."

"Hopeful about what? Did you want to get your legs worked on? Did you want to go back to work?"

"Carol, I had to want to live, first."

Carol put the phone to her chest. Outside, the dense moisture in the air was so thick it would soon freeze on rooftops, car windows, tree branches, bare bushes, power lines, and streets. The world would be sheeted ice, frozen and dead. She put the phone to her ear. "I'm not really able to talk right now," said Carol. "I'll call you when Finn gets home." She hung up, her heart as cold as the weighted sky, and sat in her chair.

When Finn walked in the back door, Carol's relief turned instantly to anger. "You weren't at mariachi practice," she accused before he'd even come into the room. "You are grounded. You're not going anywhere alone before you leave for college. Do you understand?"

"It's getting slick out," said Finn. "And I need to check on Scraps."

"Did you hear me?"

Finn sat on the arm of her chair. He put his arm around her shoulder and leaned his cold head on her warm one. "I'm home, Mom," he said. "Everything's all right."

"All right?" asked Carol. She told him about Gabriela's father on the porch.

"He won't come back in this weather," said Finn.

"Why was he here in the first place?" asked Carol.

"He wants to take Gabriela away. He probably thinks we're hiding her."

"That's serious business," said Carol. "You shouldn't be involved."

"Don't worry, Mom. Gabriela's safe. I'm staying here," he said.

"Laurence called," said Carol.

"What did he say?" asked Finn.

"Winter storm advisory," said Carol.

Finn turned on the overhead light and two lamps. "Don't sit in the dark, Mom. Laurence danced with you at the swing night. He was cool. Invite him over. You don't want him to be alone on Christmas Eve."

"That's true," said Carol.

"So call him." Finn brought her the phone.

"Come be of use," she said to Laurence, then sent Finn to the carriage house for salt to ready the porch for arrival.

Laurence was at the door so soon he must have called the cab before the invitation came.

Finn wheeled him into the house. "I smelled this wonderful place through the telephone wires." Laurence brushed ice crystals from his coat. "My impeccable sense of timing tells me dinner is almost ready," he said.

"Humble fare," said Carol. She helped him with his coat. "I boiled a chicken for the broth, so stringy meat is what we eat. A potpie."

"I smell more," said Laurence. "Is that dill?"

"Save your nose for the Christmas feast," said Carol.

Finn hung Laurence's coat on a peg.

"I can't wait," said Laurence. He wheeled to Carol and took her hand.

"You *will* wait," said Carol.

"I didn't mean it that way," said Laurence. "I meant it as a child means it: *I can't wait.* The pleasure of anticipation, you know."

Finn was still in his sweatshirt. He headed out the front door.

"I thought you were staying home," said Carol.

"It's getting really slick," said Finn. "I'm gonna put more salt down. Work up an appetite for the pie."

"There's salad, too. And I made your favorite with the extra pie dough," said Carol.

"Rollies." Finn smiled.

When Finn was a boy, they made them together, rolling out the leftover dough as thin as they could, lathering it with butter and covering it with brown sugar. Finn would sprinkle on the spices—cinnamon, cloves, nutmeg, allspice, and whatever else he fancied. They rolled the dough as tightly as they could and cut it into quarter-inch sections that flopped over onto the baking sheet, revealing sweet, spicy syrup between spirals of dough, like pinwheels—like "rollies," as Finn named them.

Through the front window, in the porch light, Finn skated across the iced porch floor. He might have been on his skateboard, that companion of his youth, the way he let himself rocket off the stairs and land on the sidewalk.

"You're very kind," said Laurence.

"Finn pulled my heartstrings," said Carol.

"Oh, dear," said Laurence, "and I hoped for that power."

"We'll see," said Carol.

"I must see Scraps." He wheeled into the kitchen and waited for Carol to follow. "Scraps," he whispered to the dog, who seemed to be sleeping. "Old Scraps," he said, and the dog raised his head. "You're a fine animal. Have been and remain so," he whispered. "Remain so," he repeated.

At dinnertime Carol went out the back door to find Finn. She stood on a sheet of ice. Through the thick darkness, she saw a light in the carriage house. She called out, but her voice drowned in the icy air. The porch stair railing, the patio, the bushes, the metal lawn chairs, and the power line to the house and to the carriage house were all slicked with ice. In the huge ash tree branches glistened, reflecting the bright floodlight she'd installed in the alley. She called Finn again, and this time the light in the carriage house went out. But so did the floodlight. And the back porch light. Carol stood in darkness. She went inside.

"Who turned out the lights?" Laurence shouted from the dining room.

Carol felt her way to the kitchen drawer where she kept emergency supplies. Soon she and Laurence had flashlights, and she lit candles for the kitchen and dining room and put dinner on the table. She carried a candle to the front door and opened it slightly. Her neighborhood was dark. Flashlight beams, as erratic as fireflies, winked through windows. "Finn?" Carol yelled. She went to the back door, which a red-faced Finn opened just as she reached for the knob.

Finn helped carry food to the table, where Laurence had parked his wheelchair.

"If you'll cook, I'll eat," said Laurence. "You have no idea what a dreadful cook I've found myself to be. Improving, I might add, but still dreadful."

"Mrs. Cross doesn't fix your meals?" asked Carol.

"Some things are better done by oneself, even if done poorly," said Laurence.

"I sure hope the lights come on," said Finn.

"We'll be fine," said Carol. "We can turn on the oven and sleep in the kitchen if we have to."

"I have to finish something," said Finn. "I guess I better tell you. Something for you. For Christmas. Out in the carriage house. It was going to be a total surprise."

"I wondered," said Carol. "How sweet of you."

"But I have a bunch more work to do. And I need the electricity," said Finn.

"I'll call the power company after dinner," said Carol. "Though I'm sure everybody in town has called already."

They ate by candlelight. Finn went for the rollies as soon as he finished his potpie and salad. Laurence wanted his rollies with milk, and Finn cleared the table on his way to the refrigerator to pour a glass. Just as Finn opened the refrigerator door, the lights came back on. Finn blew out candles on his way to the dining room. "I can work on my project," he said, setting Laurence's glass in front of him.

"Thank you, sir," said Laurence. He took a long pull of milk. "But before your project, perhaps we could read a bit of Dickens? Isn't that your custom?" The heater clicked on.

"Mom's custom," said Finn. "You guys go ahead." He went back into the kitchen.

Carol was glad to hear him clearing up. Deep down he was a thoughtful boy.

After Finn clambered out the back door, Carol recovered the forlorn *A Christmas Carol* from the coffee table in the living room, where Finn had slammed it down. "Do you want to laugh or cry?" she asked.

"Both," Laurence said, smiling.

Carol picked the laughter of the Christmas evening merriment at Nephew Fred's house, where during Blind Man's Bluff the shameless young man finds the plump sister and forces a ring on her finger. Then she read the sadness of Scrooge watching the negotiations in the rag man's den, realizing that the bedclothes, the bed curtains, and the bed sheets brought by his servants are his, stolen even as he lies dead in his quarters. "Speaking of sheets and beds," Carol said. She went upstairs to find sheets so she could make up the fold-out couch in the TV room downstairs.

When she came back, Laurence was in the kitchen, cleaning up where Finn had left off. "Thank you," she said.

"Don't look so surprised," said Laurence. "Remember, I came to help. I know you still have a lot of cooking to do for tomorrow."

"How do you know that?" asked Carol.

"Because I know you," he said.

"Your mother's a great cook, Finn." Gabriela took the last bite of the potpie. "My father and my brothers. Have they been to your house?" She sat on a cot, a blanket over her head and shoulders, another wrapped around her legs.

"Mom said your father came onto the porch. She didn't answer the door." He stood by the space heater he'd found in the attic. "I told her I'm working on a project out here. I can spend the evening with you," said Finn. "What should my project be? She'll ask about it tomorrow."

"I don't think about anything but the baby. And my birthday," said Gabriela. She stood up and went to the loft window. They'd not cleaned it, so nobody could see in through the grime of dirt and flies and the leavings of the birds who nested in the peak of the roof just above the small window. "They weren't sure when the baby would be born," Gabriela said for what seemed like the hundredth time. "They examined me. They asked a lot of questions. I couldn't tell them all they wanted to know."

"Because you don't want to, or because you really don't know?" asked Finn.

Gabriela sat back down on the cot. "Don't be like my father and brothers," she said. "Don't care who the father of my baby is."

"I don't," said Finn.

Gabriela reached for his hand. "I have an idea for your

mother. And my *tía* needs to know I'm okay. Send your Mr. Marble for your trumpet, and he can tell Teresa I'm well. Practice something to play for your mother. Something you make up."

Finn sneaked inside to call Mr. Marble from the upstairs telephone while his mother was busy in the kitchen. Laurence was entertaining her while she cooked her pies. The huge turkey sat on a platter, stuffed and ready for the oven.

Finn whispered a greeting into the telephone.

"My young man," said Mr. Marble. "I hope all is well."

Finn explained the errand: Gabriela's news and the silver Bach.

"Ice still coats the streets," said Mr. Marble.

"You'll have to get out in it tomorrow," Finn said. "You're invited for Christmas dinner here."

"I've been out in worse," said Mr. Marble and hung up before Finn could thank him.

Finn waited upstairs for a time. He found some lined music paper and wrote some notes he'd try on his trumpet. *Slow and martial*, he thought. Above his tentative line he wrote "Fanfare for Carol Dickens." He folded the sheet and stuffed it into his pants pocket. He was eager to hear his notes. He'd work out the timing and write variations. His mother would not be so hard to please.

A vehicle in the alley crunched the ice that was already falling from tree branches and telephone lines. Finn looked out his back window. Mr. Marble went into the carriage house, trumpet case in hand, then hurried back out. Finn went quietly out the front door and ran to the carriage house and Gabriela. "Any news?" he asked. Gabriela had moved the space heater to the edge of the cot. Her hands were stretched over the orange filaments. "I can't get warm," she said.

"Let's go inside," said Finn. "My mom would be okay with you."

"I wish we could," said Gabriela. "But I've told you before. My father and my brothers, they'll be watching. They've been threatening my aunt. If they know I'm at your house, they will bring the police and take me away. Your mother could get in trouble."

Finn nodded.

"You haven't told her, have you?" asked Gabriela.

"She'd probably bring in all the agencies and social services and school counselors. The people who deal with us juveniles." He was keeping Gabriela a secret for the right reasons. He opened the trumpet case and pulled out the silver Bach his father had given him for Christmas. "I wrote a little something already." He shook his head, still not believing the gift his father had given him. "Sweet," he said, as he had each time he held the horn. He warmed the mouthpiece, put it in the trumpet, and played into one of Gabriela's pillows to mute the sound. The notes he'd written sounded fine. He played them until he had them in his head, made a few variations, then put the horn away.

"I wish I still played," said Gabriela. "Last year is like tons of years ago."

"I've always *wanted* things to change," said Finn. "I remember the year my dad left. That was my first time for a big change. After I got used to it I understood that's what life is all about. Things change. People change. You *have* to change. Unless you're my mother, with her Christmas traditions."

"Or my father and his church and his pride," said Gabriela.

"They'll change when they have to," said Finn. He told her how Laurence's life had suddenly changed from standing to seated.

"I remember him from the swing night," said Gabriela. "I liked watching him."

"He's in there keeping my mother distracted. He wants her to fall in love with him."

"Would she marry him?" asked Gabriela.

"I don't know," said Finn. "They've been friends for years. Do you marry someone you've been friends with so long? Can it just change into something more?"

"I don't know," said Gabriela.

"How did your mother meet your father?" Finn asked.

Their parents were neighbors, in their village in Mexico. One day a carnival came and settled for a stay just outside the village on a flat place by the river. They put up a huge Ferris wheel, and they let the girls of the town ride for free, accompanied by one of the carnival hands. The town soon found out why. The carnival men below stopped the seat with the girl in it at the highest point of the wheel, and the man who accompanied her would comfort the girl in her fear, hugging her, and worse. Soon all the young women of the town were forbidden from the wheel. Only Gabriela's mother, Catarina, had not had a ride. She sneaked away to the river. Roberto watched her and sneaked after, and when the seat stopped so high, the men shouted up that the wheel was broken. Soon Roberto heard Catarina's insistence that she not be touched and finally, a scream. Roberto climbed the wheel as though it was a ladder, and when he came to the top, he climbed into the seat. He did not try to harm the man with Catarina. Instead, he looked out over the whole town and said, "*Qué vista, ¿no?*" and the wheel began to rotate. "He was a gentle man back then," said Gabriela. "Before all the children. Before my mother died from an infection soon after I was born. Before we came to the United States, and finally to Kansas."

"Maybe he will become a gentle man again," said Finn.

"I don't know any gentle men. Except you," Gabriela said. "Play for me once more, to practice for your mother."

Finn did.

"When will you go inside?" asked Gabriela.

"It's Christmas Eve. Mom's busy cooking, as usual. Maybe Laurence is reading Dickens to her. My mom's favorite."

"You are lucky to have traditions," said Gabriela. "We decorate the house. Go to church. Abuela cooks. She is a wonderful cook. But your mother's food. So different for me. Yes, a gift."

At last, Finn left Gabriela. He went inside through the front door and sneaked his trumpet up the stairs.

Laurence was in fine spirits. "We're not having a white Christmas," he said. "We're having a clear Christmas. I'm dreaming of a clear Christmas," he sang. He sensed that Carol wanted to clean up and finish cooking by herself, so he went into the dining room for *A Christmas Carol*. He read stave one and then the end. "Have you counted the semicolons in this?" he asked, yawning. Carol poured them wine, and they went to the living room.

"That would be sacrilege," said Carol. "If I were a dentist I wouldn't pull Finn's teeth to study them."

"It never hurts to look closely at what we love most," said Laurence.

"And what would that be for you?" asked Carol.

"For a long time, that would have been myself."

Carol sipped her wine. "Really," she said.

"Really." Laurence wheeled closer to Carol's chair. "Until the accident, I was the center of my own small universe," he said. "Now I have no center."

"You sound discouraged," said Carol.

"I'm not," said Laurence. "But in the big scheme of things, I don't matter much. And that's fine. Because it means that you, Carol Dickens, are as important as I am, as is Finn, as is everyone. All of us 'fellow-passengers to the grave,' as Dickens wrote." Laurence leaned closer. "But fellow-passengers need fellow-passengers," he said.

"Let's have a nice Christmas," said Carol. "Isn't that enough?"

"I'll go home tomorrow, as soon as we open presents," said Laurence. "But I must warn you. I have more than the *first* day of Christmas taken care of."

"Meaning?"

"Meaning that perhaps I will celebrate the twelve days of Christmas this year." He finished the last of his wine. "Now I'll wheel myself off to bed."

"I wish Finn would come inside. He's taking so long with his project," said Carol. "And the day after tomorrow, he'll be gone. To Arizona, with Caldwell. Then off to Macalester."

"But first, he'll finish his project," said Laurence. "I can't wait to see what tomorrow brings us from the carriage house." Laurence wheeled himself into the TV room.

Carol finished her wine slowly, then corked the bottle and put it away. She checked on the sleeping Scraps, then took a last look at the kitchen. Everything was ready for Christmas.

Carol was putting on her coat to go find Finn when he came down the stairs to check on Scraps himself. "Remember when his fur was so thick and bristly?" he asked. He went to the refrigerator for milk for Scraps' bowl. The dog lapped it up with a gray tongue. "Looks like he might make it until I get back from Arizona."

"Might," said Carol. "A big might."

"Where's Laurence?" asked Finn.

"I made up the fold-out couch. He's tired, he said."

"Me, too," said Finn. "Happy Christmas Eve. I'm glad you invited Laurence."

Finn remembered all the times he'd been unable to sleep, anticipating what Santa Claus—the generous guy with the big lap, the reindeer, the chimney skills—might put under the tree for him. Now he thought of nothing but Scraps and Gabriela. When the one might die, the other give birth. Gabriela was to turn on the carriage house light if she had pains. Finn set his watch alarm to wake him up in an hour. He'd check for her signal. If the carriage house was dark, he'd set it for the next hour, and the next, until the night was over. As a child, he'd stayed up hoping to see Santa Claus, his sleigh and reindeer in silhouette against the moon. This Christmas Eve he worried that he'd hear Scraps moaning. Or see a wan light that would signal the beginning of a new life.

stave four

presents and presences

christmas day, december 25

Carol set her alarm for the middle of the night. She thought she heard Finn's alarm, then suspected she was anticipating her own. She went to the kitchen and put the turkey in a slow oven, then returned to bed. She liked nothing better than waking slowly on Christmas morning to the rich aroma of a baking bird.

Instead, she was startled by the blast of a trumpet. Finn, in the upstairs hall. Had he already been downstairs and found the silver Bach under the tree? He played short, clear notes—up then down then back up—and Carol felt like a queen being awakened by court musicians. After the first clean phrase Finn elaborated with triplets and flutterings, moving high and low, but always returning to the royal sound at the end of the phrase. Then, after jazzing the music with bends and high notes that fell instantly to the bottom of the scale, Finn repeated his original melody.

"Wonderful!" Carol shouted. She hurried out of bed and put on a robe. "Majestic." She threw open the window to see a clear morning, the sky almost white with light. Ice dripped everywhere, as silver and liquid as the horn she'd bought for Finn, as the notes he'd played on the new trumpet. "That was such fun," Carol said as she opened the door.

Finn stood in the hall, silver Bach in hand, smiling. "My project," said Finn.

"Well, it was beautiful. Do you have the music written out?" Carol gave him a hug.

Finn hugged her back. He went to his room and brought out the nest they'd found in their forlorn Christmas tree. The woven collage of sticks and scraps was full of little pieces of paper, on each a musical note. "I call it 'Fanfare for Carol Dickens,'" said Finn. "All the notes are there."

"You arranged them wonderfully when you played." Carol took the nest. "Like birds, singing a song."

"For you," said Finn.

"Your music has always been a gift," said Carol. "How did you guess I'd be giving you the silver Bach?"

"What?" asked Finn.

"The silver Bach. You haven't thanked me." She started down the stairs.

Finn ducked past her and took the stairs two at a time.

Laurence sat in his chair at the bottom of the stairway. "Something told me it was time for Christmas," he said. He put his fingers to his ears. "I turned on the tree lights. Come see."

Finn hurried past him, but he was too late. The silver Bach in his hand, from his father, matched the new silver Bach from Carol, gleaming in its case under their sorry tree.

Carol went back upstairs. Bright light streamed through her bedroom window. Just moments before she'd been comforted by the sun; now the brightness did nothing but expose. She should have talked to Caldwell about Christmas, but he might have insisted on his giving the extravagant gift anyway.

166

"I couldn't know," said Finn through her closed door. "Can I come in?"

"Of course," Carol said.

Finn opened the door. Carol sat on the edge of the bed, and he sat next to her. "I really didn't know. And I'm sorry. I know how much you wanted to give me something really nice." Finn put his arm around her. "You always said it's the thought that counts. Really, it's so cool that both you and Dad had the same thought."

Carol tried to smile. "That doesn't happen much these days."

"It must have happened some, back in your early days," said Finn. "Like when you had me?" Finn put his hands in his lap.

Carol and Caldwell had not agreed on many things. "When two minds think the same good thought about someone's happiness, it's a fine thing," said Carol. "It's a Finn thing." She took his hand. "I love you," she said.

"Love you, too, Mom." Finn stood up. "I played my big present for you," said Finn, "but there's more. Let's go downstairs."

Carol stood up. "Let's have Christmas," she said.

They went back down. Laurence sat next to the tree. Carol looked for the trumpet, but couldn't find it; no doubt Laurence had shut the case and wheeled the gift to another room. Finn rummaged through the packages until he found one for Laurence and one for his mother. Carol unwrapped *Dickens' Christmas: A Victorian Celebration* by Simon Callow.

Laurence sputtered. "In there," he said, pointing. "Find the package I brought for you, Finn."

Finn found another book-shaped, book-heft package. "Really?" he asked.

"Indeed," said Laurence. "Even though you've been resisting your mother's attempts at the Dickens Christmas. For memory's sake, Finn. Because we never forget. And for the future, too, for all your Christmases to come."

Carol paged through her copy. "It's very nice, Finn. Thank you."

Finn tore the wrap off his copy of the same book. "Stereo books."

"Great minds, your mother's and mine."

They stopped for coffee and rolls and the small bit of sausage Carol had not used to enhance her stuffing. Remarkably, Scraps ate one, too. Matt Groner had said the dying dog could eat whatever he fancied.

After breakfast Laurence opened the book Finn had bought him, an anthology of contemporary writers, each of whom Laurence insisted he'd been meaning to read. Finn had bought Carol a scarf, and Carol had bought him the usual: socks, a flannel shirt, and a couple of gift certificates. She'd not expected Laurence to be there, so she'd written Laurence's name instead of Finn's on a restaurant certificate. Finn would be going to Arizona with his father, after all, then coming back for final exams and graduation, and then leaving for college.

"I don't have a fanfare, Finn," said Carol. "But you have those rather large packages to open still."

"I hope I know what they are," said Finn. He tore into them like a kid, tossing the paper to the side. "Yes!" he said when he'd exposed the carry-on suitcase. "All right!" he said when he tore the paper off a soft briefcase. "Cool!" he said when he popped a toiletries bag from the last of the paper. He put them on the couch. "I know you don't want me to go. To Arizona, I mean."

"Probably not to college, either," Laurence interrupted.

"Quiet," Carol hissed.

"That makes these even more thoughtful, Mom." Finn hugged her.

Carol smiled over Finn's shoulder at Laurence.

Finn gathered his presents together and started up the stairs. "Guess I'll pack for tomorrow," he said from the landing. "Then you know I have to go check on Gabriela."

"On Christmas Day?" asked Carol.

"Babies get born on Christmas, you know," said Finn.

"Obviously," said Laurence.

Finn climbed the remaining stairs.

"He's barely here," Carol said to Laurence.

"He'll be here for Christmas dinner. Each moment brings another wonderful smell."

"Finn will hardly eat before he goes back to this Gabriela."

"Don't be jealous," said Laurence. "He's connected to something big. A friend. He's got the best Christmas of any of us."

"Better than yours would have been, I suppose," said Carol.

Laurence wheeled over to her. "I love your Christmas," he said. "But Finn is making his own Christmas story. It's not yours, but that's fine. Maybe he'll help Gabriela, maybe not. But he's trying."

"I wish he'd let me in on his story," said Carol.

"You have your own Christmas story." Laurence reached for her hand; she let him have it. "And it's sustained you."

"What are you getting at?" asked Carol.

"Let Finn make his own story. Let him go."

Carol pulled her hand away. "The best advice is the hardest to take," she said. "Otherwise, you'd take mine."

"Who knows but what I might," said Laurence. "Right now, I want you. But, as you keep reminding me, I don't have a leg to stand on."

Carol had to smile at Laurence's pun. The back door slammed. "I hope he knows what he's doing."

"He's wise for his age. He made a song for you. A melody.

Such a song was once called a *wise*. He's done something for you in the midst of all he's going through. That's wisdom, isn't it?"

"I suppose so," said Carol.

"Would it be wise for me to give you a gift?" asked Laurence. "I didn't forget you this Christmas, you know." He wheeled to the tree and reached for an envelope he had secreted in the lower branches. He brought it to Carol and presented it with a flourish. "I hope this is the first of many gifts. That you'll allow me to keep giving what I can."

Inside the envelope was a certificate stating, "Laurence Timmons Has Given the Dickens House Museum, At No. 48 Doughty Street in London, a Donation of $100 in the Name of Carol Dickens."

"You sent them a check?" asked Carol.

"I sent them my credit card number," said Laurence.

"Thank you," said Carol. She kissed his cheek. "I have a special surprise for you, too, but it won't be today."

"How much do I get my hopes up?" asked Laurence.

"As high as a chimney," said Carol.

"Ah, hints and clues. To increase anticipation. The wise man waits patiently, but I am not a wise man. Keep hinting."

"No," said Carol. "I have to cook."

The turkey was browning nicely under aluminum foil. The juices were beginning to flow, the fat to glisten. They would eat at two o'clock. Carol took the broth from the refrigerator. She gathered the rest of her ingredients, the Cornish hens to stuff with oyster dressing, the russet and sweet potatoes, the onions to caramelize, the oranges and apples, the mixed nuts and olives. Her mouth watered. Laurence wheeled his chair into the kitchen doorway, *A Christmas Carol* in his lap. He began to read from where Scrooge goes to his nephew's for Christmas dinner:

"Thank'ee. He knows me," said Scrooge, with his hand already on the dining-room lock. "I'll go in here, my dear."

He turned it gently, and sidled his face in, round the door. They were looking at the table (which was spread out in great array); for these young housekeepers are always nervous on such points, and like to see that everything is right.

Laurence put the book down. "One semicolon," he said, "but you wouldn't know it to read it aloud. When you read aloud, only one class of punctuation is important."

"What is that?" asked Carol.

"End punctuation: question, exclamation, period."

"I tried to end it with you," said Carol. "But I seem inadequate when it comes to that kind of punctuation. Let that be your hope."

"While I hope, may I help you?" asked Laurence.

"Stay out of the kitchen," said Carol. "Go read your contemporary writers. I'll be surprised if you notice any flourishes of punctuation at all."

Laurence disappeared, and Carol busied herself. Cooking was magic, not only for the transformation of ingredients into food, but in how it took her mind away from Finn's absence, Laurence's expectations, her own unsure future. She followed the needs of the kitchen. After checking and rechecking, after messing and cleaning, after preparing and cooking, after putting things off and timing them perfectly, she was only minutes from dinner. The gravy began to bubble; the dilled beans were at room temperature; the pickled beets were in a cobalt blue bowl; the sweet potatoes were twice-baked with caramelized onions and black olives; the russets were mashed and waiting, still hot, in a covered dish; the turkey was cooling so that it might be carved without falling apart; the Cornish hens flanked it on either side, like minions.

Carol removed the dark sausage dressing from the turkey into one bowl, the light oyster dressing from the hens in another. All was ready, and still no Finn.

Christmas Day Feast
Menu

Chicken Broth

INGREDIENTS

Chicken, set to boil with onion, celery, garlic, thyme, salt, and
  pepper

Boil chicken. Use meat to make a potpie for either the day before or after this feast, to which you will add other leftovers. Use broth as below in the recipes.

Turkey with Sausage Dressing

INGREDIENTS

Turkey, 1, so large it looks as though it could never have stood
  on its legs
Butter, generous
Salt, generous
Pepper, generous

STUFFED WITH

Pork sausage, ground and browned
White bread, 2 loaves, left out the night before to dry, then
  cubed
Celery, 6 stalks, chopped
Onions, 2 large, chopped
Poultry Seasoning, to taste

Eggs, 2, beaten well
Chicken broth, 1 cup or more

Mix the first 5 ingredients together, then moisten with egg and broth until the stuffing holds together but is not doughy. Stuff turkey. Melt butter and add generous amounts of salt and pepper. Rub into and over the turkey. Put in roasting pan on rack and bake, uncovered, in 450-degree oven. Reduce heat to 350, cover, and bake for a total of 20 minutes per pound of turkey. Baste occasionally. Uncover again at the end, to crisp the skin. Let stand at least ½ hour before carving. Remove stuffing to a bowl to serve.

Make gravy of the drippings, adding flour to brown in the fat, then more of the chicken stock, salting and peppering to taste. Kitchen Bouquet can darken and flavor turkey gravy if you like that option.

Cornish Hens with Oyster Dressing

INGREDIENTS
Cornish hens, 2
Butter, generous
Salt, generous
Pepper, generous

STUFFED WITH
Oysters, 2 tins
Bread, 1 small white loaf, dried, then cubed
Celery, 2 stalks, diced
Garlic, 6 cloves, minced
Eggs, 2, beaten
Chicken broth to moisten

Prepare dressing as above, only using Oyster Dressing ingredients. Stuff hens and bake in 425-degree oven for 15 minutes, then turn heat to 350 and bake for an additional hour. Remove, let sit, carve at table, putting stuffing in separate bowl. Smother in sauce (see description, page 133).

Dilled Beans

INGREDIENTS
Water, ½ cup
White balsamic vinegar, ⅓ cup
Brown sugar, ¼ cup
Salt, ¼ tsp.
Pepper, ½ tsp.
Dill, 1 tsp., dried
Allspice, 3 seeds
Green beans, thin, 1 lb.

Bring all ingredients but green beans to a boil, then turn to low to simmer. Wash and snap green beans, steam until just tender—still bright green, no touch of gray. Run cool water over green beans and put them in a flat pan that has a lid. Pour on hot dill sauce, seal, and leave to marinate. Can be reheated or served cold.

Pickled Beets

INGREDIENTS
Beets, small, 1 dozen
Cinnamon, 2 sticks
Cloves, 1 dozen whole
Nutmeg, ½ tsp., ground
Fennel seeds, ½ tsp.
Salt, ½ tsp.
Garlic, 1 head, minced
Vinegar, ¾ cup
Water, ¼ cup
Sugar, to taste

Cut off beet tops, leaving an inch of stem and the root, and boil beets for 15–20 minutes, until the skins slip off easily. Immerse in cold water, skin the beets, then slice them thinly. Put all other ingredients in a bowl, stir, then add beets. These beets will taste better the longer the flavors mingle, so prepare in advance by as much as a day or two. Serve cold or reheat.

Mashed Potatoes (*see recipe page 62*)

Twice-baked Sweet Potatoes

INGREDIENTS
Sweet potatoes, 6
Onions, red, 2, caramelized
Peppers, poblano, 2
Lime, 1, juiced
Paprika, smoked, to taste

Bake sweet potatoes, remove from skins, put in baking dish, and cover with onions and poblano peppers, roasted and cut into strips. Sprinkle lime juice, then paprika over top and bake until everything is heated through.

Appetizer

Serve an assortment of olives and nuts.

Dessert: Fresh Fruit

Grapes, orange slices, Granny Smith apple slices, pear slices (and whatever else given taste and availability) arranged on a platter.

Dessert, continued

If you need more dessert than fruit, make a traditional pumpkin or pecan pie.

Drinks

Serve dinner with Beaujolais Nouveau and a good Chardonnay. Serve the fruit plate with Grand Marnier.

"This is my strangest Christmas ever," said Gabriela. She paced the carriage house attic, stopping to stare into the dusty window. "I miss my *abuela*."

"Bet you always got some presents, too," said Finn.

"Not many," said Gabriela. "What I *needed*, not what I *wanted*. My *abuela* would fix a huge meal. That was her gift. Tamales, even better than Rosaria's. Rice with peas and onions, cooked with tons of butter. And her guacamole. So good."

"My mother's meals are gifts, too. I'll miss them," said Finn. "I don't know what I'll miss about my father."

Gabriela turned from the window. Nobody could see in, and she couldn't see out. "Every Christmas my father says, 'I take care of you. That's my gift.' After my mother died, I don't think he had anything left. He could take care of me, but he couldn't *give*."

"My father gives gifts *instead* of taking care of me."

"Your father is helping me," said Gabriela. "And you're taking care of me. That's your gift."

"That's not all the gift," said Finn. He ran down the attic stairs and came back up with the trumpet his father had given him. He set the case on the bed. "For you."

"You can't give me this," said Gabriela. "What would your father say?"

Finn took the trumpet out of the case. "He won't ever know," said Finn. "My mother gave me one, too. Same silver Bach. You should have one of them. Teresa wants you to play in the mariachi band. And I'm leaving for college." He handed her the trumpet.

Gabriela stroked the trumpet like a pet. "Over and over, I think the same thing, like a song that won't leave my head. When I'm eighteen, I'll do what I want. Nobody will have power over me or my baby."

"Just four more days of being illegal here," said Finn. "Starting tomorrow, I'll be here with you. I've been hoarding food. I'll stay until the baby comes or until your birthday, whichever comes first."

"My birthday, I pray." Gabriela put the trumpet away. She stretched out and held her belly.

"Pains?" asked Finn.

"Nothing important," said Gabriela. "I will live with Tía Teresa. We've planned that. I'll go back to school and graduate, like you. Teresa wants me to go to college."

"And the baby?"

"She wants me to give up the baby for adoption. In that, she's like my father. The Birth Center people can help, if that's what I decide."

Outside, melting ice dripped from trees. Sometimes pieces cracked against the roof of the carriage house. "You think you'll give the baby up?" Finn walked closer to Gabriela.

She looked away from him, at the wall. "It might be best to start over," said Gabriela. "Let someone else love this baby in case I cannot."

"Are you going to tell who the father is?" asked Finn.

"No," said Gabriela.

"Everything has to be a secret?" said Finn. "Maybe we should just tell the truth."

"Do you want to tell your mother?" asked Gabriela.

"Yes and no," said Finn. "Yes, because I usually do. No, because she might take over. She gets these notions in her head, and that's the way it has to be. Right now she's in the kitchen making more food than anyone can possibly eat. We always eat it for weeks afterward. She calls it the Twelve Days of Christmas. I call it the Twelve Days of Leftovers."

"We'll be happy to have the extra food while we wait," said Gabriela.

"We will," admitted Finn. "But my mom not only fixes food, she fixes everything. If I told her, she'd try to get you to make up with your father. Or she'd do the official thing. She's not like Mr. Marble."

"Don't be mad at her for wanting to do what's right," said Gabriela.

Finn took her point. "What do you think your mother would be doing right now?"

Gabriela stood up. She put her hand to her mouth, as though afraid to say anything. She moved to the window and back again to the cot, then to the window again. "You're so sure what your mother would do," she said finally, "and I'm so unsure what my mother would do. I wish I had known her better."

"What do you wish she'd do?" asked Finn.

"I wish she would love me," said Gabriela. She sobbed quietly.

"I'm sorry," said Finn. "I really am."

"You've helped me, Finn," said Gabriela. "I don't expect you to love me, you know."

Finn looked at his watch. "I'd better get inside," he said. "And sit through this huge meal, and bring as much as I can back to you. Are you hungry?"

Gabriela smiled, though her eyes and face were red from crying. "My appetite is coming back."

"I'll bring you a ton," said Finn. He went down the stairs and out the side door of the carriage house. He was locking it up when Mr. Marble's face appeared around the corner, then disappeared. Finn followed him into the alley.

Mr. Marble crouched next to a leafless bush. "You're smart to lock it, and keep it locked," said Mr. Marble. "Right now our own Caldwell Dunmore is driving my truck around town. 'Meander,' I told him, 'maybe the bastards'll run out of gas.'"

"My father in your truck?" Finn asked.

"Indeed," said Mr. Marble. "In deed, he's not such a bad fellow. He cares about you."

"Why is he driving around?" asked Finn.

"And on Christmas Day of all days?" asked Mr. Marble. "Roberto Diaz and his sons are stirred up. I spoke to them, see, tried to calm them down, but they only became more suspicious. They threatened me, as though I knew where the young woman was, you see. And when I asked them if they'd reported Gabriela as a missing person, they said nothing. I pressed them, I had to, until they said it was not the business of anyone but family."

Finn nodded.

"I'll be going, young fellow. Best of luck to you."

"Only a few more days," said Finn.

"You're an expert on labor and delivery are you, son?" asked Mr. Marble.

"No. But Gabriela turns eighteen on the twenty-ninth. Teresa will pick her up."

"Your mother thinks you'll be in Arizona. Where will you go?" Mr. Marble put his hand on Finn's shoulder.

"Once Gabriela turns eighteen, I'm telling my mother all about this."

"Good idea." Mr. Marble squeezed Finn's neck. "Your mother's a fine woman."

"You're invited to dinner, you know," Finn reminded Mr. Marble.

"Not today," said Mr. Marble. "I'm a suspect, you see. Can't be seen here. Don't want to make your mother one, too."

Finn hurried into the house. He hadn't realized how hungry he was until he opened the back door and Christmas dinner—or perhaps the accumulation of so many Christmas dinners, all the memories of smells, tastes, textures—overwhelmed him, bringing unexpected tears to his eyes.

"Perfect timing," said Carol as Finn came in the back door. "Are you all right?"

"Happy to be home," said Finn. He kissed her on the cheek. "Where's Laurence?"

"Waiting, of course," said Laurence from the dining room. "Nearly succumbed to appetite and anticipation. I've carved the roast beast, and it simply sits here, like me, waiting to be of service."

"Then let the feast begin," said Carol. "Unless you think Mr. Marble is coming. You did invite him?"

"He can't come," said Finn. He carried bowls to the table, and more bowls, and more.

The turkey was moist, so succulent that the gravy, rich and brown and salty, would have been unnecessary except that it tasted so good. The potatoes, mashed with cream and butter, might have been a meal in themselves, but they were accompanied by their sweet counterparts, dressed with the sweet onions, poblano strips, and, Carol's last touch, sprinkled with lime juice and paprika. The Cornish hens were so tender they would not be cut; the meat fell from the bones as if surrendering. And the oyster dressing—that hint of the sea, of England, of common ancestry with Charles Dickens—might have been a pudding it was so rich when spooned from the insides of the hens. The sausage dressing, savory with sage and onion, complemented the gravy and the turkey and was the dark twin to the oyster dressing, equally rich and vying for attention. The vegetables, beets with roasted garlic and dilled green beans, though exotic, though perfectly sweetened, roasted, pickled, were like second thoughts—but the kind of second thought that elaborates so well the primary thought that one could not exist without the other.

As they ate their way through each dish, then dabbled at second helpings, and then thirds, Laurence blessed each dish forkful by forkful, mouthful by mouthful, swallow by swallow. "I never," he said, beaming.

"I ever," Finn teased him. "Every Christmas." He smacked his lips, imitating Laurence's obsequious pleasure.

Carol beamed. If the Christmas season hadn't been what she'd expected, at least the meal was fine. Maybe Finn was like her, with an ability to be transformed into the moment by food. "More," she said, encouraging Finn and Laurence.

"After you," said Laurence, and of course she had to set an example.

They ate and drank the wines Carol had set out—just a sip in each glass for Finn—and, after they could eat no more, they spent another quarter of an hour reliving the meal through story, as though it were an epic that would swell their stomachs in memory if they recounted it enough times.

And still there was pie, pumpkin and pecan, thin slivers of each, with whipped cream and, for Finn, chocolate sauce. Finn had a hero's appetite. Laurence's appetite was declaration of appreciation—not only for the food, Carol thought, but for her invitation, for her company. She smiled at each bite of dessert he took. And her appetite? She keened for more than food.

The meal was all she'd hoped it would be. Enough to sustain her through Finn's absence for a week, and then his going away to school, through her last negotiations with Caldwell, through whatever decision she made about Laurence. Maybe Laurence was right: appetite, desire, pleasure, only momentary things, were key.

They cleared the table. Finn took leftovers to Scraps, "For old times' sake," he said. Then he went to his room to finish packing.

Laurence, true to his word, called a taxi and waited by the front door. Carol almost asked him to stay, but his resolve in keeping his word promised other resolves. "I leave you to Finn, and then to yourself," he said as the taxi pulled into the drive. "But expect another day of Christmas tomorrow."

Carol was intrigued by his suggestion of more. She washed the dishes, stashing a refrigerator-load of leftovers into the nooks and crannies of that already-stuffed appliance. When she went upstairs to check on Finn, he wasn't in his room. She called down the stairs. No answer. She checked the upstairs attic, then the basement, suspecting he might be doing some last-minute laundry. He had disappeared. She climbed back up the stairs to his room. The luggage she'd given him lay on his bed. Had he packed already? She unzipped the carry-on suitcase. On the top was a thin blanket; under that, wool socks, jeans, sweatshirts, and underpants; under those, a box of graham crackers and some tins of sardines and Vienna sausages. No shoes. No T-shirts.

An hour later Finn opened the back door as quietly as he could. "Sorry," he said when Carol appeared from the kitchen. "I went to Gabriela's one last time."

"You forgot your bag," said Carol.

"My bag?"

"I saw what you packed. That's not for Arizona." Carol studied her son.

Finn fidgeted. "Right," he said finally. "Turns out she doesn't need those things. She was going to run away. Now she's not."

"And you?" asked Carol. "Are you running away?"

Finn shook his head. "I'm taking a trip, but I'm not running away." He hugged her. "I love you, Mom," he said. "I've had the best Christmas ever."

Carol smiled.

"I'm going up to pack, for me this time, for Arizona," said

Finn. "Then try to sleep for a little while. Dad's coming by around midnight, remember?"

Carol nodded. "I'll stay up." They went into the living room.

"You don't have to," said Finn. "He won't come in."

"I know," said Carol.

"You want me to pour you some wine?" asked Finn.

"I think I've had enough," Carol said.

"It's Christmas, Mom," said Finn.

"That'd be lovely, then," said Carol. "I'll read the Simon Callow book you gave me." She sat in her favorite chair.

Finn brought her a glass of wine from the bottle they'd not finished at Christmas dinner. He found the Victorian Christmas book—hers or his, he wasn't sure. He started up the stairs, but then he turned around. "I'm sorry I didn't get you more. For Christmas," he said.

"You've been occupied with your friend," said Carol. "Maybe I should get used to that. You're going to be part of a bigger world than . . ." She paused, searching for words. She'd almost said *bigger world than me*, but that sounded self-pitying. "Bigger world than Topeka," she finished.

Finn bounded up the stairs.

Carol settled in with the book. She was soon fascinated by Callow's history, his spirit of Christmases past. She'd had hers, too. The terrible disappointment with her father. The London Christmas that rejuvenated her celebration of the season. And now this one, soon to be past when the clock struck twelve. She read and thought and finished her glass of wine. She poured herself another. And read more. At some point she pulled the book to her and fell asleep. When she jerked awake, she felt an odd stillness. A note rested on the arm of her chair. "Didn't want to wake you up. Love you, Finn."

Carol went to the door and peered into the night. Finn was gone. She wished Freda were in town. She had so much to talk about. Should she call Laurence? No, he'd promised her a tomorrow. She went to bed and tried to find sleep once more.

friday, december 26

When she awoke, Carol felt the emptiness of the house, then remembered Scraps. The dog had drunk some water, but the leftovers Finn had given the dog were untouched. Scraps winced at Carol through glassy eyes. When he tried to move, his diminished weight listing, then settling again into weakness, she called Matt Groner's office. The phone rang and rang. Finally a breathless voice answered.

"Is Dr. Groner in today?" Carol asked.

"I'm just feeding and exercising. He's not in until Monday," said the voice.

"But Scraps," said Carol. She stopped herself. "I'm sorry," she said. "My dog needs some attention. Matt said I should call him in an emergency, like before I start the hydration and morphine."

"Did he show you? Usually he shows people," said the voice.

"Yes," Carol admitted. "I'm just not sure it's time. But the dog is whining."

"I'll have him call." The woman took Carol's name and number.

Carol went back to the pantry. "It'll be all right, boy," she said.

As though to prove her right, Scraps lapped some water.

Carol hadn't counted on Laurence, but she was happy when he knocked on the door. "A gift," he said and handed her a package.

She invited him in. She opened a long rectangular box to find a pair of oddly colored gloves—a hideous aquamarine, the kind of blue Carol remembered from the sugary cereals Finn once craved. She swallowed as though trying to rid herself of the taste of Fruit Loops. "Thank you," she said.

"Maybe they'll come in handy," Laurence said, winking.

"They will if I ever put—or should I say 'pun'—them on," said Carol, attempting to match his wit.

Laurence stayed for lunch. Carol complained about the quiet, empty house. They spoke of the weather. They checked on Scraps, who was asleep, deep breaths thinning and flaring his nostrils. By the time Laurence called a cab Carol felt steadier.

"Might I return tomorrow?" he asked.

"Unless you want me to come there," said Carol.

"That would be wonderful," said Laurence.

As soon as he left, Carol called Freda. To her relief her friend did not seem otherwise occupied. Carol explained the events of the past several days. As she spoke, everything seemed more normal to her. "I miss you," she said. "I wish you were here."

"Take it from me," said Freda. "When you're alone, you discover a great deal about yourself."

"What have you found out?" asked Carol.

"More than I can explain over the phone. We'll have a wonderful meal when I return. In two weeks. Merry Christmas."

"Merry Christmas." Carol hung up the phone.

By the time Matt Groner called, Scraps had eaten a small amount of leftover turkey and a dog treat. "I want him to hang on until Finn gets home from Arizona. Is that too selfish?"

"Keep in touch," said the veterinarian. "I'll let you know when I think you're being selfish."

saturday, december 27

Carol spent Saturday at Laurence's house. She felt guilty leaving Scraps, but the dog seemed no different, and Carol needed a change. She took wine and leftovers. She cleaned Laurence's kitchen, though it was not the mess she'd faced before. "Mrs. Cross?" she asked.

"I sacked her a week ago," said Laurence. "I'm doing for myself."

"Congratulations," said Carol.

"I have something." Laurence wheeled into the living room and brought out three slim packages. Books, from the looks of them. Carol sat down and opened them. They were three different versions of *A Christmas Carol*. The first was published in 1980 by Samuel French. "The dramatic version," said Laurence. "From my own collection."

The second was a French translation, *Un chant de Noël*, with 175 illustrations, including forty-five "lost" engravings. "The Doré illustrations are from 1861," Laurence said. "This was the first book appearance for them, since before then they'd only been published in a French periodical. Look inside, in the back."

Carol opened to what was a bibliography.

"All the publications and illustrations in the history of *Carol*."

The third of the books was, again, *A Christmas Carol*, the Candlewick edition, abridged by Vivian French.

"Abridged?" asked Carol.

"In case you're in a hurry. Traditions to-go," Laurence teased.

"You're very thoughtful," said Carol.

"And you're not *thinking*." Laurence held up his hand against her forthcoming protest. "There's a message in all this," said Laurence.

Carol tried to read his mind. "Here we come a-caroling? *A Christmas Carol*-ing?" she asked.

"Very good," he said. "But no. You have two more days to figure it out."

"You're making no sense," said Carol.

"Ah, we seem to be at loggerheads again." Laurence pointed to a bowl of dried rose petals.

"The roses, with their days of meaning. The weird gloves yesterday, these editions of *A Christmas Carol*." Carol made a face. "I don't need gifts. You were going to start making things different for yourself."

"More bargaining, Carol? I make changes for you, and *then* you'll begin to feel something for me? I don't think it works that way. Certainly, love doesn't work that way." Laurence wheeled close to her. He reached for her hand, and she gave it to him. "I do have more up my sleeve."

"What?" asked Carol.

"Let's eat," said Laurence.

They ate another lunch of leftovers. Carol tidied the kitchen, corked the wine, and prepared to leave.

"Stay," said Laurence.

"Scraps," she said. "I've already been gone too long."

"Tomorrow?" asked Laurence.

"Tomorrow is Sunday. My day of rest," said Carol. "Actually, I need to work."

"Then take the envelope on the stairs," said Laurence. "Open it tomorrow."

sunday, december 28

After checking on a lethargic Scraps, Carol opened the envelope from Laurence. In it lay four old-fashioned cards, what society people called "calling cards." She read the names on them: Charles Dickens, William Makepeace Thackeray, Cedric Dickens, Jane Austen. They were brittle and yellowed. Were they actually real, from the times of these authors? If so, how much had Laurence paid for them? And how could she match gratitude to expense during this transition in their relationship?

Carol puzzled out Laurence's gifts. He'd given the Dickens house a rather generous donation. He'd given her the Dickens books. The calling cards had a Dickens connection. But the gloves? Was she missing a reference to oddly colored gloves in Dickens, perhaps in one of his other Christmas books or in some of the short fiction she'd never read? Did she want to admit defeat by asking Laurence for an explanation? Should she call him? Visit?

She had determined to work. She brought together her books

and camped on a chair in the kitchen by the pantry door. Sometimes she read from her books aloud so that Scraps could hear her. Her day of counting punctuation was punctuated only by more leftovers. She began to think Scraps could last through the week.

She had included one more American, poet Emily Dickinson, and how appropriate this day, reading to Scraps: "Because I could not stop for death . . ." Though Carol had predicted Dickinson might be in a class by herself, she actually seemed to follow the pattern established by the English authors. Carol counted: in her early work, the first ninety-nine poems of the First Series of 1890, there were twenty semicolons; in the Third Series, those of 1896—nearing the turn of the century—Dickinson's final 175 poems contained just eight semicolons.

The phone rang. Carol picked it up. "Just me," said Laurence, "your friendly calling card. That's a joke, by the way."

"You must have spent a great deal on those cards," said Carol.

Laurence laughed. "Carol Dickens? Deliberately punning? Cards? And great deal?"

"Unintentional," Carol confessed.

"What are you doing today?" Laurence asked.

"Counting punctuation. Reading Emily Dickinson aloud to Scraps. 'I heard a fly buzz—when I died—.' Slightly macabre."

"What editions do you have?"

Carol told him and reported on the semicolon usage.

"If you're including Dickinson, you need access to the original drafts. After her death, all the editions were brought out by editors who didn't understand her punctuation at all. Those dashes. They regularized her. They had you in mind, giving you more semicolons to count."

"Really?" said Carol.

"Really," said Laurence. "You don't have to know everything. You haven't figured out my gifts yet."

"Ha!" barked Carol. "Gifts of the last few days, or your general gifts?"

"Try for both."

Scraps whined, and Carol said good-bye. She abandoned Dickinson as one more complicated American, though if editors had regularized her poetry with semicolons, that still reflected the time period, the conventions of the nineteenth, rather than the twentieth, century. She could debate that with Laurence, though she preferred to contemplate his gifts, small and large.

monday, december 29

Quiet had its advantages. Scraps slept. Carol ruminated. She sat in a chair imagining her gift to Laurence even as it occurred. Carol could see him sitting, as was his custom, in his bay window, his wheelchair locked, coffee mug on the table next to him, a stack of books—what he called his "tower of good intentions"—next to the coffee. Before he'd lost his legs, Laurence had been a voracious reader. Almost every week he would come to work excited about a "discovery," a "great" novel, a "must-read" author. He exhorted Carol to read more. He always said he meant to garden, or to walk the trails along the Kaw River, or play golf with his friend Mick, or take long car trips to climb mountains or descend into canyons. Instead, he read books. "Now that books could be my solace," he told Carol after his accident, "they stack up like the mountains I'll never climb."

This day, Carol knew, he sat in his chair, a lazy cat in his lap, staring into the blue sky of December, into a chilling brightness that exposed the ugliness of his brown-leafed oak tree, his pocked driveway, his short picket fence peeling paint. His coffee would be cold by the time he remembered to drink it. Would he take the trouble to wheel into the kitchen to heat it? He would read the titles of the stacked books and wonder how he'd thought he might ever read them.

Then, as Carol had planned, he'd see an old truck wandering down the street. The rack on the back of the pickup would be festooned with ladders, buckets, long-handled brushes. And when the truck pulled into Laurence's drive, he would see the driver, an old man in a small hat with a red feather, frizzled gray hair springing from beneath it. The truck's door would be decorated with a top hat and brush with the simple word *SWEEP* below it. The old man would open the door, jump nimbly to the driveway, and Laurence would have to wheel to the door to answer the persistent bell. He would reach forward to the knob, swing the door open, and back away in his chair.

"Remember me?" the old man would ask cheerfully. "Harry Marble." The old man would open the screen door and step in. "Time you had a fire, good sir. Take the chill off December."

"I didn't send for you," Laurence would say. His chair would no doubt block Mr. Marble's passage into the house.

"Still, I am sent," Mr. Marble would say. "In the spirit of a Christmas present, sir. Now show me to the fireplace."

Laurence would let him in, and Mr. Marble would check the damper, and go outside to climb the roof, and do his magic with brush and bucket, and secure the chimney cap, and clean the firebox with broom and Shop Vac, and find the rotting woodpile, and supplement the soft wood with some good oak from the back of his truck, and grab the sports section of the *Topeka Capital-Journal* from the passenger seat and start a fire to check the draw of the chimney, and, when the wood caught, he'd sit by the fire, Laurence now wheeling close to the hearth. And, as Carol had directed him, Mr. Marble would say, "Now everything is cricket."

Surely Laurence would remember Dickens' Christmas novel, *The Cricket on the Hearth*, about the older man with the young wife who loses confidence that he is his wife's one true love, even that he is lovable at all? In the end he is restored to confidence and sits at last content in front of his own hearth, crickets chirping his very happiness. To cement the association, Carol had asked Mr. Marble to deliver a little metal cricket, which he would take out of his pocket and place on the brick hearth. The piece was made so cleverly that the metal expanded and shrank in response to the fire, making clicking and scraping sounds, almost cricket-like, almost real.

Carol waited by the telephone, waited for *that* chirp, waited with the hope of warmth. She waited through half the morning before she heard anything in her still house. A terrifying whine came from the pantry, high-pitched and awful, as though all the pain Scraps had contained through the last several days had found its way to his throat. The dog moaned, grunted, heaved, choked, and whined again. Carol was frightened to go to Scraps. But she did. Then she ran to the phone.

"I don't know what to do. I don't think he'll let me near him," Carol said when she finally got hold of Matt Groner.

"I'd better come," said the vet. "Sounds like he's telling us it's time."

"Please," said Carol. She hung up. Why did Finn have to be gone? She paced the floor, remembering what she'd heard others describe. She would hold Scraps. Dr. Groner would give an injection. She'd feel Scraps lose his grip on life, loosen into her arms. Then what?

Groner arrived. Scraps seemed to know him, seemed to understand his mission. Matt Groner gently scooped the dog into Carol's lap, the dog's weight insubstantial, as though he'd finally become the small scraps he'd been named for. Groner readied the needle, reassured Carol, made the injection, wrapped his arm around Carol's shoulders as the dog went limp in Carol's arms. She wept without shame. She wept for Scraps, for Finn, for herself. She had a moment of panic, for she was truly alone in her house for the first time since Finn had left for Arizona. But she wiped her eyes and lifted Scraps onto his blanket.

She fixed Matt Groner a cup of tea. Though she dabbed at her eyes, she still salted her tea. Matt told her the stories of others who had experienced the same process. "I can take care of the disposal," he said finally.

"No," said Carol. "Even if it's against the law, Scraps will be buried in the yard."

"The ground is frozen."

Carol hadn't thought about that. "Damn," she said.

"I've known people to keep a pet in the freezer and wait for warmer weather," said Matt. "I'd offer to take the body for storage, but I'm not allowed to."

"I could put him in the carriage house," said Carol. The old outbuilding was the coldest place she knew. Even in the middle of summer the building felt air-conditioned, with its thick stone, its earthen floor, its dusty windows. The attic loft absorbed the little heat that sparkled through the huge cottonwood tree someone long ago had failed to cut when it was a sprout against the south wall. The tree roots had actually worked their way through the stone foundation and up into the dirt floor of the old place. The tree branches spread over the rotting roof, with its flaking shingles and sagging joists.

"As long as you get the body in the ground as soon as possible," said Matt.

"Finn will be back on New Year's day."

"I can carry Scraps to the carriage house, if you'd like." Dr. Groner stood up.

Carol shook her head. "I want to do it."

Matt nodded, put his teacup in the sink, and left the house.

Carol sat alone, wondering when she'd be ready to pick up her dead dog. She almost called Laurence, but in less than a month, when Finn left, she'd do everything by herself. For years Finn had mowed the grass, taken out the trash, cleaned windows, raked, picked up fallen limbs, shoveled snow.

Carol would adjust to the change. Just as she wanted Laurence to adjust to his. Would he get fitted for prostheses? Return to work? He had already begun to change self-pity into generosity. If he continued his progress, she would give him the attention he wanted. Could he accept such a bargain?

After all, he had not bargained with her in the year or so after Caldwell moved out. He'd only supported her. Should she do the same for him? And without a price? She could hear Finn. "Bad Who," he would accuse her. Christmas was not about exchanges but about spirit.

Only good spirits would get her through this transition. She went to the kitchen drawer where she kept the carriage house key. She couldn't find it. Where had she put it? She put on her coat and went outside. Maybe Mr. Marble had left the carriage house open.

A car pulled into her driveway. Mr. Marble climbed out and walked toward her. "Going somewhere?" he asked.

"You're just the man I need to see. I can't find my key to the carriage house."

"Just one moment," said Mr. Marble. "Your friend is with me."

Laurence waved. She realized where she'd seen the automobile before. Laurence's aging Audi, his former wife's car, mothballed in his garage, "appreciating in value," Laurence always said.

Carol sighed, her breath a vaporous cloud so visible she wished she could take it back.

"Could you give me a ride back to my truck?" asked Mr. Marble. "I had to leave it at Mr. Timmons' house. Cleaned his chimney, just as you asked. Such a nice fire he wanted to share it with you, he did." Mr. Marble started down the drive.

"No," said Carol. She went to the Audi and explained the situation to Laurence.

Laurence took her hand. "I'm so sorry about Scraps," he said. "I know how you must feel. And now I show up. And I've imposed on your Mr. Marble."

Carol didn't know if he was apologizing or asking for her help.

"The car is for Finn," said Laurence. "It's my fifth day of Christmas present."

"Laurence," she said, "this is not a time to discuss gifts. I have a dead dog in the house. I need to get the body into the carriage house."

"I'll help," said Laurence. "But please, let's just get Mr. Marble home."

Carol shook her head. She sighed. Then she gave in. She went to her Subaru and swung open the passenger door. Mr. Marble recovered Laurence's wheelchair from the Audi, and Laurence swung into it and wheeled up close enough to Carol's car to swing himself in. Carol shut the door after him. Mr. Marble folded the chair and took it to her trunk. He slammed it shut. "Where would you like me to park the vehicle, ma'am?" he asked.

"Anywhere away from the driveway," said Carol. "Laurence and I need to talk." She couldn't let Finn have a car, such an expensive gift. They would be too much in Laurence's debt. Or should she say too much *more* in his debt? Mr. Marble started the Audi, backed up, then pulled it along the curb in front of the house. She looked it over. Red, somewhat worse for the wear, but she liked the boxy design, the symmetry of the car, the safety record. If Laurence didn't want it anymore—if he drove, it would have to be an automatic—she would buy it from him. She noticed the logo rings on the back of the trunk. Four chrome rings. She was beginning to make sense of Laurence's gifts. "If Finn is to have a car, he has to earn it."

"He has," said Laurence.

"How?" asked Carol.

"Being your son," said Laurence. "Must be a paying job somehow."

"Don't be rude," said Carol.

"Can't I give you . . . him . . . something I don't need?" asked Laurence.

"Fifth day of Christmas indeed," said Carol.

"Ah, you're starting to put things together," said Laurence.

"The Audi has only four rings, and they aren't gold."

"So I'm not perfect," said Laurence.

Mr. Marble went to Carol's porch, peered in the house, then came back to the Subaru. He opened the back door and climbed in. "How long since you've had a fire in your fireplace?" he asked.

"Too long," said Carol.

"Need a cleaning?" asked the sweep.

"Seat belts," Carol said.

Laurence put his on. Mr. Marble sat still. When Carol looked at him in her rearview mirror, he said, "I don't normally bother with a belt."

"If you want to ride with me, you don't have a choice," said Carol.

Mr. Marble smiled. "Yes, ma'am." He clasped the belt around

him and saluted Carol. "I've done it, I have," he said. "Just as commanded." Carol backed the car out of the drive. They rode in silence. Carol didn't want to talk about Scraps; the sanctity of his death was now so interrupted that she felt sullied. She sighed. Laurence reached over to touch her arm, but she shook off his hand.

Carol found herself in front of Laurence's house without even thinking about getting there. Had she been missing her daily trip? She pulled to the curb. Mr. Marble was out of his seat belt and the car so quickly he might have been a teenager escaping his parents. Carol rolled down her window. "The key!" she shouted. "To the carriage house!"

Mr. Marble turned.

"I can't find mine," Carol said.

Mr. Marble, uncharacteristically silent, removed a key from a huge ring of assorted keys—and miniature knives and screwdrivers and church keys and beads and buttons. He handed it to her. She put it in her slacks pocket. He hurried to his truck.

"Your timing couldn't be worse," she said. She laid her head on the steering wheel.

"I've always thought life was more important than death," said Laurence.

"Then why won't you start living?" asked Carol.

"Why don't we both?" asked Laurence. "Enough to risk screwing up." He shifted in his seat to face her.

"Screw what up?" asked Carol. She turned to him.

"Screw up my courage. Screw up your day even more." Laurence reached into his coat pocket. He handed a little wrapped box to Carol.

"Why do I know what this is?" asked Carol.

"Because it's the fifth day of Christmas?" asked Laurence.

"No. Because you've been asking me off and on all month.

Because you've been in cahoots with Finn. Because you've been so attentive. And generous. But honestly, a car?"

"It's the fifth day of Christmas. It's all I could think of. The Audi has four rings. You're holding the fifth," said Laurence. "The golden ring."

"I know," said Carol.

"So open it," Laurence urged. He clasped his hands together.

"Do I have to say yes or no?" asked Carol.

"Only if you say *yes*. If it's *no*, you can wait."

Carol unwrapped the box. In it rested a golden ring, thick, etched with two lines looping around each other. The spaces between the lines were just big enough for the letters C and D and L and T.

Laurence pointed. "We could put a date in this space here. Sometime. After the prostheses. So I'll have some legs to stand on?"

Carol closed the box. She was fighting tears. "Scraps is dead," she said at last. "And Finn is gone. I have to carry a dead body to the carriage house." Carol put the ring box in her purse. "And right now!"

"Can I be with you?" asked Laurence.

She answered by pulling into the street and heading home.

"I'm sorry." He shook his head. "I can wait. As I've waited through these first five days of Christmas."

"Five golden rings," said Carol. She tried not to think about Scraps. "I get that. And the four calling cards. That's your idea of four calling birds."

Laurence broke into song. "Five golden rings, four calling cards, three French ones, two turquoise gloves, and a charge card toward your favorite charity."

"Very good," said Carol. "I didn't get the French ones. And

turquoise gloves? Very good. How soon are you going to rehab?"
She pulled into her driveway, recovered Laurence's chair from
the back, watched him swing himself into it, and pushed him up
to her porch steps. She reversed his chair, leaned it back, and
pulled up. He was strong enough to turn the wheels, helping lift
himself up the three stairs. "Rehab?"

Laurence, breathing hard, did not answer her.

"Or were you waiting for my answer first?" asked Carol.
She opened her front door and pushed Laurence into her cold
house. "We'll talk," she said. "After I get Scraps to the carriage
house." In her front closet she found an old blanket. She went
to the pantry, covered Scraps in the blanket, and hoisted him
up. She hurried out the back door and nearly ran to the side
door of the carriage house. She put the body down.
Mr. Marble's key opened the rotting door, and she stepped inside. The carriage house was a musty place, eerie, too, with the
gnarled cottonwood roots like snakes on the dirt floor. She
could put Scraps' body anywhere, really. The place was dank
as a tomb.

She turned to pick up Scraps; a small beam of light pene-
trated a crack in the attic floor. She slowly climbed the stairs.
Someone had put a lamp in the attic and left it on. *Finn*, she
thought, *when he was working on the music*. But at the top of the
stairs, Carol saw everything: cot, space heater with red coils
glowing and fan whirring, two sleeping bags, Finn's backpack
and luggage. Last, she saw a dark stain on the soft attic floor-
boards. She ran down the stairs. She placed Scraps' body on the
earthen floor and hurried back inside the house. She flew to
where Laurence had parked himself in the living room. "You
knew, didn't you!" she shrieked.

"Knew what?" he asked.

"You knew Finn was in the carriage house."

"I guessed," Laurence said. "Then I asked Mr. Marble. This morning. You could have guessed, too. You could have asked."

Carol found her purse, rummaged for the ring box, and held it out to him.

Laurence put his hand over hers and squeezed hard. "Don't be angry," he said. "Let's go to them."

"Where are they? Her water's broken. It's all over the cot and the floor."

"Gabriela's having the baby!" Laurence exclaimed.

"At the hospital?" asked Carol.

"I don't know where," said Laurence. "But Mr. Marble said Finn will call."

"How did they get to the hospital?" asked Carol.

"Is the Audi still in front?" asked Laurence.

Carol went to the front window. The Audi was gone. "You bastard," she said. "I'm taking you home."

"Please," Laurence said. "This is Mr. Marble's conspiracy, not mine. Though I must admit I admire that old man."

Carol put her arms in the air and shrieked again, the same terrible sound coming from her as had come from Scraps earlier in this terrible day.

Laurence held up palms to quiet her. "The way I understand it," he said, already wheeling himself toward the front door, "is this. If you had known, then you would have been breaking the law. Nobody wanted you to be implicated."

"I'll remember that," said Carol. "Why should I be implicated in anyone's life."

"Not what I hoped you'd say," Laurence said.

"Hope isn't something *you* should hope for," said Carol. "Not now." She slammed the door behind them.

They left as they'd come in. Laurence shoveled himself into

the Subaru. She drove recklessly, careening around corners, speeding. His house was no trip at all, really.

She pulled into the driveway, slammed out of the car, opened the trunk, and pulled out Laurence's chair. Laurence had opened his car door and was ready to swing into the chair. "I'll find my way up and in," he said, not looking at her. She slammed the car door behind him. "Before you harden your heart against me, or Finn, or Gabriela, or Mr. Marble—"

"My God," said Carol, "am I the only one left out of the plan?"

"Join the plan," said Laurence. "It's Christmastime. For God's sake, open your heart. Finn didn't set out to hurt you. He needs you more than ever."

Carol had spent the past seven years making a wonderful celebration of Christmas, that season of togetherness, of food, of warmth, of decoration, of rich tradition. Only to be abandoned once more: father, then husband, now son. Even the dog. Each had devised an escape. She drove home.

Carol called the hospitals and described her situation. Nobody could help her. She could not remember Gabriela's last name, so she couldn't call her father—what was his name? Roberto, Finn had said. She hurried back to her car and headed to Oakland. Maybe she would see Roberto, or his car, the rusted Pontiac that had been in her drive the day she refused to answer the door. Should she have spoken to Roberto that day? Carol drove straight to Our Lady of Guadalupe Church. She parked the car and walked into the priest's office. "Roberto," she said, "and his daughter, Gabriela, who is pregnant." The priest took her to the door and pointed down the street.

"The small house there," he said. "Look for some new steps on the porch. The new landlord just built them."

"Thank you," said Carol. She started away.

"Ma'am?" said the priest.

Carol stopped and turned.

"Your business with Roberto Diaz and his family? He's had a rough time."

"I have, too," said Carol. "I simply need to speak with him." Carol found the house with the new porch steps. She climbed them and knocked on the door.

The man she'd once seen on her porch opened the door. He did not invite her inside. "I need to know where your daughter is," Carol said through the screen.

"My daughter," hissed Roberto. "She is no longer my daughter. She has betrayed me and my family. She is gone. She does not listen to me. She does not obey." He opened the screen and came out on the porch. From his worn jeans he took a tin of chewing tobacco and put some in his mouth. Immediately, he spat into the brown grass. "She does not do as I tell her, not like in Mexico. There, a daughter respects a father. Here, they are all whores, listening only to the boys. She was *mine*." Roberto's breath came in billows of spirits and tobacco. "She has spoiled herself. If I knew where she was, I would go to tell her these things."

"Thank you," she said quickly, and as he muttered after her, she nearly ran to her car. *Monster*, she thought to herself, *as though a parent owned a child*. She jerked down the street, hoping he would not follow. Halfway home, she began to cry. She wanted her son.

She parked her car in the drive. The Audi was still gone. She went straight to the carriage house. Nobody was in the attic. Carol left a note. "I love you," she wrote. "Let me help, too." She went inside.

She thought about calling Caldwell. He'd been part of Finn's plan. But she did not go to the phone. By now, nobody could tell her what she hadn't already figured out. Besides, her life had nothing to do with Caldwell anymore. And although she loved Finn to bursting, her life was her life with and without him, too. Carol sat in her chair and waited for Finn's call, the one Laurence had promised her. She sent hope and prayers to Finn and Gabriela.

Finn woke Gabriela early in the morning singing "Happy Birthday." This was the day he'd take her to her *tía*, Teresa. Gabriela stretched and sat up, smiling. Then her expression changed to one of wonder. Her hand went to her womb. Finn couldn't believe the amount of fluid: it stained Gabriela's smock-like dress, it flowed onto the sleeping bag and off the cot onto the floor of the carriage house attic. He swallowed hard, but then Gabriela said, "It *is* a birth day. They told me to come right away. They told me not to worry. That this might happen."

Finn hurried down the stairs and silently thanked Mr. Marble when he saw a car, an Audi, in front of the house. He went to the mailbox for the key, where the old man said he'd leave it. By the time he started the car, Gabriela appeared with a bag stuffed to overflowing. She waved, walking slowly to the car, holding herself. Finn jumped out to open the door for her. Once she was inside, he raced down the street. His hands trembled on the steering wheel. Gabriela reached for him. "Don't worry. Now, everything is all right."

Finn could not fathom the source of her sudden confidence. He was sweating. She sat staring straight ahead, a distant smile on her face. He barely stopped at intersections, gunning the motor through the turn on to Sixth Street, weaving impatiently through slow traffic, turning almost wildly into the parking lot at the Birth Center. He parked at the back, near the alley, and

hurried to the rear door, where he knocked loudly and continued knocking until Maria opened up, glanced briefly at Gabriela,
and asked, "It's time?"

Finn held Gabriela's elbow, helping her up the back steps and
inside.

"We can have a bed ready soon," said Maria. "Both birthing
rooms are full. But we have a room in the back."

Finn looked into a tiny room off the kitchen. "This?" he
asked.

Maria nodded. "Go to the waiting room. Time the contractions."

"We don't have a watch," said Finn.

"Clocks," said Maria over her shoulder. "In every room.
We're interested in time. So time them."

Finn and Gabriela found two chairs in a waiting room nearly
full of family members who had grouped themselves close to the
birthing room doors. Each set of them took turns staring at Finn
and Gabriela—sometimes with sympathy, sometimes with what
looked like disapproving pity. Finn ignored them. "Have you
had a contraction?" Finn whispered.

Gabriela nodded, her lips pursed. "The pains began a while
ago."

"You're not screaming," said Finn.

Gabriela smiled. "I'll scream later, if you want me to. For
now, I can time my own contractions. Go call Teresa."

"We already have," said Maria, sticking her head in the door.
"And happy birthday!"

Finn and Gabriela waited. Dr. Drewland rushed between the
two birthing rooms, then finally took Gabriela to the small room
at the back of the center. Finn sat in the waiting room for what
seemed forever, then Maria stopped to whisper in his ear, "You

can go in any time." Finn met Dr. Drewland in the hall. "Could be a long wait or a short wait," she said. "With first labors, usually long."

Finn and Gabriela looked at the magazines stacked next to the bed. Finn had never seen a copy of *American Baby* or *Parents*. He was amazed by all the questions, concerns, studies, products, projections, reports, and paraphernalia. Occasionally, he tried to show something to Gabriela. "I never look at what I'll never have," she said. Finally, he showed her a picture of a baby. "I'm looking," she said. After half an hour, Gabriela nudged Finn. "Go tell them my contractions are very close together." Finn ran through the kitchen. He nearly bumped into Mr. Marble. "Wha . . . what . . ." he began.

"I saw your car, the Audi," Mr. Marble said.

"My car?" asked Finn.

"Now I've ruined a surprise," said Mr. Marble. "Not that it matters at a time like this. You see, your friend Laurence asked for my help, and when help is needed I like to be there. I delivered a vehicle to your house, as promised. But it's also a gift, you see. Good little car, that one. Quite a present." Mr. Marble looked past Finn and through the door. "Everything all right here?" Mr. Marble pointed to the waiting room.

Before Finn could answer, Gabriela gasped, then moaned. "She's back there," said Finn. "She sent me to get the nurse." Maria came from the front hall. Behind her, Teresa waved. "The contractions are really close," said Finn.

"Stay in there," Maria said, nodding toward the waiting room. She and Teresa went through the kitchen to the makeshift birthing room.

Finn found the chair in the large waiting room where he'd sat earlier. Mr. Marble took the seat next to him. "Tell me all about your music," said Mr. Marble. "And that fine new horn you sent me for."

Finn talked about trumpet, how he'd taken to music, how he wanted to study it and play it and compose it and do things nobody else had ever done with brass music, which, as he explained, didn't need to be just two things: military-style marches or jazz, either cool or hot. The mariachi music of Mexico moved the trumpet between percussive syncopation and plaintive melody, a sound he hadn't thought to make. He wanted to study music from everywhere, play music from all over the world. Someday he would find a new sound the trumpet could make. That was what he wanted for his future, Finn told Mr. Marble.

The old man clasped Finn on the shoulder. "You are a strong young man, Mr. Finn. Headstrong, too. Like your mother."

Finn rolled his eyes.

"Where is she, your mother?" asked Mr. Marble.

Finn looked down.

"You promised," said Mr. Marble. "A strong man does not go back on his promise."

"It's not quite time," said Finn.

"Did you see them rushing back there?" asked Mr. Marble. He craned his neck comically, as though his head could find its way down the hall without his body.

Gabriela's moan made its way through the kitchen, the hall, and into their ears. Finn had a single moment of complete bewilderment. He'd imagined all of this, almost from the beginning. He'd seen Gabriela that night when he was out walking, and he'd imagined helping her somehow. Imagined protecting her from her father. And then from his own father, once Caldwell put her house up for sale. He'd imagined getting her into caring hands that knew about pregnancy and birth. And here he sat, and she was about to have her baby, and he'd done what he set out to do, and it seemed so much to have done, with all his planning and secrecy and hiding and scavenging and determination. But he was nothing, really. Gabriela and her child were everything.

And once his mother knew, the whole thing wouldn't quite be *his* anymore. "Can we wait until we know everyone's okay?" Finn asked Mr. Marble.

"I simply advise," said Mr. Marble.

Gabriela screamed Finn's name. He started up from his chair and hurried down the hall. Maria was in the kitchen. "She's fine," said the nurse.

"She called me," said Finn.

"Stay here," said Maria. "Women frequently cry out."

"God, God, God, God!" screamed Gabriela from the tiny back room.

"You see," Maria said, smiling, "she's calling on everything she knows. Don't worry, she's doing fine."

From the last time Finn had been at the Birth Center, he knew the anguish, the loudly expressed pain, of childbirth. This time he felt faint with the force of it. "Tell me if anything bad happens," said Finn.

Maria touched his arm. "Women have been having babies for a long, long time."

Finn retreated to the waiting room. Laurence Timmons sat next to Mr. Marble. "Sorry," he said to Finn. "Took a while to rouse a cab."

"How did you know?" asked Finn.

"My car . . . your car . . . was missing. I knew Mr. Marble would tell me where to find you. I almost called your mother. She knows most everything now, anyway." Laurence motioned to the seat next to Mr. Marble.

"I told the young man to call," said the chimney sweep. "But it's his decision."

"I want to wait until I know everything is all right."

One of the families in the waiting room was taking turns sneaking into a birthing room to ogle a newborn. The tiny cries, gurgles, and grunts filled the air.

"Yes, sir, a baby changes everything," said Mr. Marble, "as tiny as it is. See those folks tiptoeing in and out? See them smiling and whispering? Quite something, isn't it?"

"I never had children," said Laurence.

"I was the old man in the shoe," said Mr. Marble. "Had so many I didn't know what to do. Now they're grown and scattered. Like most kids. And the woman who labored for each is gone, too. Scattered, but with a different meaning, if you catch my drift."

Laurence nodded. He wheeled a bit closer to Finn. "Scraps died today," he said. "Just so you know. The body's in the carriage house. Your mother wants to bury him in the yard."

Finn put his hand to his mouth. He'd known Scraps would die, as surely as he knew Gabriela would have her baby. Both left him stunned.

"Maybe I shouldn't have told you," said Laurence.

Finn's eyes stung, and for more than Scraps. He let his tears pool, let his eyes swim in the richness of all that had ever made him happy and sad. An hour, maybe more, passed, punctuated by Gabriela's voice, sometimes moaning, sometimes screaming. The sky dimmed, then darkened. The other mother had her baby, and that family tiptoed in to see. The waiting room was a tide, people were pulled in and pushed back out. Finally, some of them left.

Laurence yawned and yawned. Finn paced. Mr. Marble reached for his hand when he was close. "They don't like to come, most of them," said Mr. Marble. "They like swimming, all safe and sound, in their mother's womb."

Maria came to the door. "Baby boy. All is well," she announced. "Gabriela wants to see you, Finn."

Finn nearly ran to her room. Gabriela lay propped up on pillows, her baby already at her breast, trying for some milk. "You're okay?" asked Finn.

Gabriela nodded, tears in her eyes.

"All has been well for some time," said Dr. Drewland. "We've been cleaning up. And we've been talking."

Teresa stood silently in a corner. Finn went to the bed and sat down. "Have you decided?" he asked Gabriela.

She shook her head.

"You have no say in this," said Teresa. "Unless you are the father of this child."

For a moment, Finn wished he *were* the father of Gabriela's baby. They'd all thought he was anyway. Hadn't Teresa warmed to him beyond what he could have expected, and let him play with her band? Hadn't Roberto Diaz punched him and threatened him? Hadn't old Juan celebrated the pregnancy with him and told him to care for Gabriela and the baby? Hadn't her godmother, Rosaria, welcomed him to her restaurant the first time he'd had lunch there with Gabriela? Could he just say that the baby was his, and change his plans to leave for college, and figure out what to do from there? He took a deep breath.

"Finn is not the father of my baby," Gabriela said flatly. "I alone have to decide. I'm eighteen years old. Nobody can tell me what to do."

"Even if you are living with the mistakes you made at seventeen?" asked Teresa.

"I need a moment with Gabriela," announced Dr. Drewland. "Final examination." Finn and Teresa went to the waiting room.

They found two arrivals. Laurence had called Caldwell, and Finn's father had brought Gabriela's godfather, Juan, *el ciego*. "Only your mother is missing," said Laurence.

"And Gabriela's father," said Teresa.

"Can we wait until morning?" asked Finn.

Nobody answered him. In the odd assortment of family and friends, awkwardness descended. Their ears were cocked for sounds from Gabriela or the baby; mother and child were the only thing that joined them, connected them, wove them together. "Such a tiny little boy," said Teresa. "So tiny and so perfect."

Caldwell and *el ciego* slipped out the door.

tuesday, december 30

Carol, in her favorite chair, had fallen into a deep sleep. Uncomfortable, and slightly chilled with no blanket, sleeping with an awareness of being both asleep and awake, she dreamed of dogs, babies, blankets. She heard whining and barking and laughter, she slipped on ice, spilled a water bowl, found a pool of punctuation and musical notes that sounded static, then silent, then static again, until they were in a bowl, then a nest, then disappeared like frightened birds. She counted in her sleep: punctuation and notes, but also the sevens of sins and muses and dwarfs and musical notes, and the dozens of disciples and eggs and roses, until the pink and white and yellow and then blood-red petals all fell to the floor, and she lost count, and she was lost and felt she was drowning in all the things she saw and heard and counted, and she thought she heard a knocking, a door knocker, Marley's face from *A Christmas Carol* appearing suddenly to haunt her, and she heard the knocking again, and as she rose from her drowning dream, she shouted, because she did not know who she was, or where she was, and even as the knocking continued she reached for the window curtain to pull herself up out of her dream, out of her chair, and the curtains fell around her, smothering her. She screamed again, flailing until she found her way out of the fabric. And she woke, and she was herself again, and she was in her chair, in her living room, in her house. She was not drowning, not smothering. She breathed deeply and stood, letting the curtains fall to the floor. She went to the door. She recognized the tall Hispanic man with the white cane. He seemed to look everywhere and nowhere. "Carol Dickens?" he asked.

"Yes." Carol came out on the porch. Dawn was still hours away. "Do you know where Finn is?" Carol asked.

"With our Gabriela, of course," said Juan. "Come." He held out his hand.

Carol took his worn brown hand in hers. "Should we take my car?"

"Yes, my ride has already left me," he said.

"Thank you for coming," said Carol. She pulled him inside. Her house. Dark, but her furniture, her chair, her rumpled curtains, her coat, the promise of her son.

"I promised you," said Juan, as though he could read her mind.

She slipped into the coat and grabbed her purse and keys. She took Juan's arm and led him to her car. As she helped him into the passenger seat, she was surprised to find him quite limber.

When Carol was seated, Juan turned to her. "You go this way some blocks," he pointed south, "and then a turn to the right. A busy street, a corner with a light. A restaurant is nearby, Mexican. You will be looking for a big house. A parking lot, too. No grass nearby."

Carol backed out and headed down the street as fast as she dared. "Sixth Street?"

"You are probably correct," said Juan.

She went the few more blocks and turned right. As soon as she was on Sixth, she remembered the birth clinic in the old brick house on the corner of Sixth and Washburn. *And so close by*, she thought, as she saw it appear in the streetlights of Topeka. She swung into the parking lot and jammed on the brakes.

"You knew where you were going?" asked Juan.

"*You* knew," said Carol. "And I remembered." Carol wanted to run inside, but she went at the old man's pace across the lot and through the door. And down the hall. And into a room so full of surprises her body actually swayed. Juan felt her sudden weakness and held her arm tightly. The baby was the least of the surprises, for she'd known there would be a baby. And Gabriela. And Finn.

But Caldwell was there. And Laurence, smiling up at her from his chair. And Gabriela's Aunt Teresa. And Mr. Marble, who came to her and took her hand. "We were just ready to call you," he said. "But Mr. Juan beat us at our own game. Welcome."

"Welcome?" asked Carol.

"This is a welcome party," said Mr. Marble. "There's been a baby born, you see. In the middle of the night. Right here." Mr. Marble took off his hat, the one with the tiny red feather in the band, and swept it expansively, including each person in the room.

"And?" asked Carol.

"Thank God you're here," said Laurence. "Finally." He wheeled to Carol and pulled her toward Gabriela, who lay on a couch, baby in her arms. Carol sat next to her, still shocked. Finn beamed at her.

"Everything went great," he said.

Carol pulled down the corner of the blanket to see the tiniest nose and mouth, a proliferation of brown hair, tiny hands that played with the air for a moment then settled again. Carol looked into Gabriela's eyes, the same eyes she'd just seen in the baby's face. Tears welled up. Were they for the newborn? Or for Finn, who was safe? And Gabriela, safe, too? She wiped her tears and stood up. "Thank you for bringing me," she said to Juan. Then she sat back down before she fainted.

Caldwell soon took his leave. He had a plane to catch, to Arizona. Mr. Marble left, too. Carol asked to hold the baby—as yet unnamed, they explained, given the decisions to make. Finn stood behind Carol, his hand on her shoulder, and what a reassuring touch it was to her. Teresa sat next to Gabriela on the couch, rubbing her niece's hands, her arms, her shoulders, as though touch were her only sense. Juan sat on one side of the door, Laurence on the other: they were either guards, or ready to make quick escapes, Carol wasn't sure.

"Decisions?" Carol asked finally.

"About the baby," said Finn.

"Adoption," said Teresa. She approached Carol as though to wrest the baby away.

"Tía!" said Gabriela.

Finn moved quickly in front of his mother. He carefully cradled the baby to him and put it in Gabriela's lap, a bold move for a young man unfamiliar with babies.

"Tía, I don't know what to do," said Gabriela.

"This baby is yours," said Teresa. "But yours and who else's?" When Gabriela began to sob, Teresa sat next to her on the couch again. "It is time to tell me, child."

"I can't," said Gabriela.

"You must," said her aunt.

"I will tell, without names," said Gabriela. All her reserve, all the secrecy, all the hiding, seemed to overpower her. She gasped and held her hand to her mouth. She took a deep breath. "Last

March. During our spring break. Remember, I went to the music camp. We stayed in dormitories. My first time away from home. There was a boy, and I liked him. I let him stay in my room the last night we were there. I didn't want to give in to him, but I did. I prayed I would not become pregnant, but my prayers were not answered. School would be out before anyone needed to know."

"Why won't you tell the name of the boy?" asked Teresa.

"Because it was *my* fault," said Gabriela. "I won't make him pay like my father has made me pay." Gabriela's tears splashed on the infant's face.

Finn went to Gabriela's side. "Do you think the boy would want to know?"

Gabriela smiled up at Finn. "Only you would think that way. I never heard from the boy again. Most boys feel trapped. They look guilty, like they're in a police lineup. I didn't want a lineup. I wanted a boy like you, who would stand up for me."

Juan began to sing, "*Cuando tratamos a cada niño como a mi hijo, los niños serán mejores padres del mundo.*"

Teresa nodded again.

"What?" asked Carol.

Finn translated for her: "When we treat all children as our own, then children become good parents in the world."

"I will be the father of the child," said Juan, smiling proudly. He walked slowly forward until he stood in front of Gabriela. "We will *all* take care of your baby, *conejacita*," he said. "You must know that. If the baby has no father, then everyone must be the baby's father."

The baby stirred in Gabriela's arms, its little mouth in the O that would soon have a nursing blister, would soon smile, would soon gurgle and then talk.

"My father won't help," said Gabriela.

"He once climbed up high to rescue your mother," Finn reminded her.

"Now he waits at the bottom for me to fall," she said.

"Maybe he will surprise you," said Teresa. "As everyone here has surprised each other."

Carol remembered Finn in her arms all those years before, but she also remembered how many others had come forward to hold him, to bless him with their presence.

Laurence wheeled the last small distance between himself and Gabriela. He put his hand on the baby's head. Gabriela put the baby in Laurence's arms. He rested the tiny infant in his lap, his "perpetual lap," as he called it, since he could not stand. But a fine lap it was for holding a baby.

"Why so secretive?" Carol asked Finn. "I would have supported you both. I would have helped."

"We didn't want to get you in trouble," said Gabriela. "I ran away. You would have had to report me . . . or something." She looked to Finn. "Now I am eighteen. I can make a decision. To keep this baby."

Finn looked around him, at all the people gathered together, quiet now that Gabriela had announced her decision. The baby began to cry in Laurence's lap, and Laurence picked him up and rocked him in his arms.

"Mom," Finn said just above a whisper. "Remember how I used to walk and walk, at night? I'd be wondering about stuff, about my life. I saw Gabriela, and her father, and I thought *she* was the reason I was walking around. I kept thinking I should tell you, but I wanted something to come just from me. From me alone. So I could know I'd leave for college and be okay. I had to do *one* thing my way."

"I think I understand," said Carol.

"You did your one thing very well," said Laurence.

"Thank you, Finn," said Gabriela.

"You and Gabriela," said Teresa. "Children taking care of each other. Now, you will have more help. If this is your decision, it is because you know that many people will care for this baby."

"For Francisco," said Gabriela.

"So that is his name?" Teresa hugged Gabriela. "And we will care for you, my Gabriela."

Later that day, when Carol finally arrived home, she was elated and exhausted. Before she rested, she called the florist. She ordered a single rose, to be delivered to Laurence Timmons. When asked if she wanted anything written on the card, she dictated, slowly and carefully: "This rose does not count the past; it promises a singular future."

She could only imagine the expression on Laurence's face when he read the card. She hoped he would be as excited as she was.

wednesday, december 31

Finn had one regret, though Carol reassured him that his heart had been in exactly the right place. Gabriela had needed him much more than Scraps. But the next day, when Gabriela left the Birth Center to live with Teresa, Finn felt the force of his dog's death. The day was warm, and Finn tested the earth of the backyard. He dug the half-thawed topsoil without much difficulty. Beneath those first six inches, he found the earth pliable, accepting the shovel, and so he stayed with it, digging a hole three feet deep, two feet wide, three feet long, big enough, he hoped, to hold the body. He went inside where his mother had gathered some mementos of Scraps' life—the blanket that had been his bed in his final days, a rubber bone he'd nearly chewed through in several places when he was a pup, a once-green tennis ball, now black with soil and dog drool.

Together, they went to the carriage house. Finn lifted Scraps' blanket-covered body, the weight of his grief outweighing the dog, who seemed diminished in death.

"Do you want to look?" asked Carol.

"I want to remember Scraps the way I first saw him."

"You remember that?" asked Carol. "Your father and I thought you picked the worst-looking dog in the entire pound."

"I did," said Finn.

"You have good instincts, Son," said Carol.

"Scraps turned out to be a great dog, didn't he, Mom?"

"He did. A great dog for a great son," said Carol.

They went outside with the body and the gathering of Scraps' life. They laid everything gently in the hole Finn had dug. "It's hard to say good-bye," said Finn. "But you were a great dog, and I love you." Finn shoveled a spade of dirt over the blanket that held Scraps' body. He handed the shovel to Carol. Finn held back his tears.

"We can bury you," Carol said to the form of Scraps. "But we can't bury your life. We remember the good times and the bad. We thank you, Scraps, for your fine dogginess." She smiled at Finn, and he smiled back at her. "And for your dogged pursuit of life even when you were ill," said Carol. She turned some dirt into the small grave.

Finn smiled at his mother's pun. She'd been spending time with Laurence. "Here's to your bark and your bite." Finn shoveled more dirt.

"Doggone, we loved you," said Carol.

"Dog gone," Finn repeated and began to shovel dirt in earnest. Memory flooded him with the dog's touch, his loyalty, his playfulness. Suddenly, Finn felt as though he was burying more than his dog. Could you bury your childhood? He chuckled.

"You're lighthearted, for a gravedigger," said Carol.

"Scraps knows how much I loved him," said Finn. "And you

know, too. We won't forget. We'll never forget." He rested his palms on top of the shovel, put his head on his hands.

"You okay?" asked Carol.

He nodded. He replaced all the dirt. The grave was a small mound in the yard, and he and Carol went inside to plan a party.

stave five

the end of it

wednesday, january 6

On the Twelfth Day of Christmas, the Day of Epiphany, the day Hispanic Catholics call Three Kings Day, Carol Dickens and Finn Dickens-Dunmore gave a celebration. Carol had spent the day before cooking. "It'll be fine, Mom," Finn had said. But Carol ignored him. "I like to prepare feasts," she said. "I have to do it. Just as you had to do what you had to do. We can respect each other."

Finn did.

After all, Carol had her traditions. She started a Smoking Bishop, an American version, with five sweet oranges, a grapefruit, sugar—too much by any standard but the standard of a Smoking Bishop, which meant a quarter of a pound—two bottles of cheap strong red wine, a bottle of ruby port, and some cloves. She baked the oranges and grapefruit in the oven until they were pale brown and then put them into a warmed earthenware bowl with five cloves pricked into each. She added the sugar and poured in the wine. She covered it and put it in the oven where the pilot light would keep it warm.

As their guests arrived for the meal, each, like the Three Kings, brought gifts.

Juan, *el ciego*, brought all the money he'd collected during his Christmas of bringing others good luck. He put a gold dollar in little Francisco's layette "so that he might always be rich."

Laurence Timmons, the man without legs, brought a baby stroller. "Wheels from the man on wheels," he said. "And here's some oil to keep the wheels moving well. It's the best, and I may not need it much longer. I see the doctors tomorrow."

Mr. Marble brought such an array of powders and wipes and outfits that Gabriela was embarrassed. "Frankly, I couldn't stop myself," said the old man. "You get in one of those baby sections, and everything is so little and charming, and you remember when you had your little ones and how precious and temporary and fleeting baby-ness is . . . and . . . well, you spend a little time, and you spend a . . . little!"

Gabriela's *abuela* beamed her pleasure as she set the tamales she'd brought, along with rice and beans, on the table next to Carol's gifts, a repeat of the oyster-stuffed Cornish hens and sweet potatoes from Christmas. They began their feast when Gabriela's father arrived. Roberto Diaz, whose neck was pinched in an unaccustomed tie, held the baby for a moment, then gave him back to his daughter. "The hair," he said. "Like yours when you were a baby."

Caldwell Dunmore dropped in for dinner, though he did not stay long. He had just returned from Arizona. When he left, Carol finished the Smoking Bishop, squeezing the oranges and grapefruit into the wine and pouring it through a sieve, then adding the port and heating her concoction, but not so much as to dissipate the alcohol.

The Twelfth Day of Christmas
Menu

Twelfth Cake (after Brenda Marshall, *The Charles Dickens Cookbook*)

INGREDIENTS

Cherries, glacé, ¾ cup
Lemon, 1, for rind and juice
Prunes, 4 oz.
Orange, for the rind
Raisins, 1 lb.
Almonds, blanched, 4 oz.
Butter, 1¼ lbs
Marmalade, 6 oz.
Sugar, 1¼ cups
Currants, 1 lb.
Molasses, 1 tbsp.
Milk, for moistening
Flour, 1½ cups
Brandy, 2 tbsp. and more as cake ages
Eggs, 8
Salt, 1 tsp.
Allspice, cinnamon, cloves, ginger, nutmeg, ½–1 tsp. each

Chop cherries, prunes, and raisins. Cream butter, sugar, and molasses and stir in nearly ½ cup flour. Add eggs, one at a time, beating well. In a separate bowl, mix flour, spices, and salt and stir in orange and lemon rind, almonds, cherries, currants, raisins, and prunes. Add contents of bowls together with the juice of the lemon and blend well, adding milk if necessary. Put mixture in a 9-inch tin lined with wax paper, 3 or more layers.

Bake at 350 degrees for 2 hours, then lower the temperature to 300 degrees and continue baking for between 2 and 2½ more hours. Cool very slowly by wrapping it in a towel. Once cooled, pour brandy over the base of the cake. Continue daily shots of brandy until ready to consume—best if prepared a week ahead of time so Twelfth Cake is besotted by the time it is eaten.

Smoking Bishop (after Cedric Dickens, *Drinking with Dickens*)

INGREDIENTS
Oranges, 6
Cloves, 30
Juniper berries, 6
Allspice seeds, 6
Sugar, 4 oz.
Red wine, 1 bottle
Port, 1 bottle

Bake oranges in 350-degree oven until they begin to turn brown. Prick each orange with 5 cloves and put them in a bowl with juniper, allspice, sugar, and wine. Let sit for a day. Press ingredients through a sieve or strainer, add port, and heat (but not to boiling!) until smoking. Pour and enjoy!

Carol brought out this masterpiece, and the guests visited over their Christmas bowls of Smoking Bishop. They toasted one other, but most of all they toasted the new baby in their midst. They finished their fine feast with Carol's Twelfth Cake. Finn eyed the food differently, for he had no need to hoard it for Scraps or for Gabriela. He had no need to worry.

At the end of the evening Carol made a toast. She stood next to Laurence. "This Christmas has been a time of great transitions. I look forward to the new as much as I have relished the old. But, like Scrooge, I promise to always live in the present. As a baby does."

"Hear, hear!" shouted Laurence Timmons. "God bless the end of this long sentence!"

"No," said Carol Dickens. "No end punctuation. No periods." The others in the room would not understand her, but she didn't care. "Allow me to toast the semicolon." She raised her glass. "The go-between of clauses and meanings; the transition mark that tells us there is more to come; the signal that promises all shall be joined in meaning. To semicolons, used and still-to-be used. God bless them every one." She took a small box from the pocket of her blazer. "And to rings, soon to be worn."

"Worn, but not tired?" Laurence said, and smiled.

Then, from the porch, such a commotion of music, more lively than the street musicians of Dickens' time, those known as *waits*. The mariachi band struck up and clamored for entrance, and the door was flung open and music poured into the house. Finn was happy to hear the sound of mariachi, which, like all he'd experienced in the past three and a half weeks, he would carry with him into his future.

At the end of the night, Carol and Finn stood on the porch and sent their guests into the world. They looked up at a clear night of stars: Carol wondered whether stars were the sky's punctuation or if the sky, between the stars, was the punctuation. Finn marveled at the ever-turning galaxy, how it remained so constant.

Right then, of course, the sky simply charted a singular moment: when Carol and Finn's Christmas came to its end; yes, the

End.